"You heard me—I resign."

Annie stood her ground as Nick glared at her. He pointed at the chair. "Sit down."

She backed away stubbornly. "No, thanks. I don't—"

"Sit down!"

Annie sat quickly. "I won't let you bully me."

"I'm not—" Nick gritted his teeth, then drew a deep breath. "Okay, I'm calm. See how calm I am?" His voice rose. "Number one, stringers quit or they get fired, but they don't do anything as grand as *resign!*"

"I stand corrected. Now, if that's all—"

"I'm not even close to being finished with you," Nick thundered.

"Because I'm a lady, I'll try to overlook your blatant attempts to browbeat me," she said stiffly.

"Maybe you're right," Nick growled. "Maybe you should quit. Because I need a *woman* for this job, not a lady."

Ruth Jean Dale comes from a newspaper family. She herself was a reporter for years and her husband is the editor of a small Southern California daily. Even her youngest daughter works as a journalist. Ruth Jean says, ''Newspapers and newspapering were my first love, romance novels my second. Combining the two, as in *Society Page,* is my idea of heaven.''

Books by Ruth Jean Dale

HARLEQUIN TEMPTATION
244—EXTRA! EXTRA!
286—TOGETHER AGAIN
315—ONE MORE CHANCE

Don't miss any of our special offers. Write to us at the following address for information on our newest releases.

Harlequin Reader Service
901 Fuhrmann Blvd., P.O. Box 1397, Buffalo, NY 14240
Canadian address: P.O. Box 603,
Fort Erie, Ont. L2A 5X3

SOCIETY PAGE

Ruth Jean Dale

Harlequin Books

TORONTO • NEW YORK • LONDON
AMSTERDAM • PARIS • SYDNEY • HAMBURG
STOCKHOLM • ATHENS • TOKYO • MILAN

ISBN 0-373-03097-5

Harlequin Romance first edition January 1991

With thanks to Day Leclaire,
who read and read and read . . .
And to Paula Wilson,
who always gets last cut

PROLOGUE

"ADMIT IT, NICK. Annie Page is perfect for the job."

Nicholas Kimball drummed his fingers across the scarred top of the desk and frowned at Rosalind Charles, his managing editor. Roz had worked at the Buena Vista *Bandwagon* from youth to middle age, while he'd only been there for the past five of his forty years. She'd forgotten more about the town than he'd ever know.

Fortunately for her continued employment, he realized that. Otherwise, as publisher and owner of the newspaper, he wouldn't have been sitting there in his office trying to be patient while listening to her sing the same old song.

She was starting to wear him down, though, he realized glumly. He hoped it didn't show. After six months of turmoil over semiliterate social columnists, he could feel his resolve weakening.

"Anybody but Annie Page," he said in the authoritative tone he'd developed during his years as a foreign correspondent.

Roz's hands tightened on the sheaf of papers and newspaper clippings in her lap. "But—"

"No. Give it up."

She thrust out her jaw. "Okay, boss, you asked for it." She sifted through the pages, selecting one. "This is Nadine at her finest."

She began to read. "'Pulses notoriously throbbed with the sting of some articulate exposition as the sun splayed over the horizon with its rays of molted gold fanning out into a pale yellow glow that provided munificent ramifications.' "

Nick frowned. This was worse than he'd anticipated; he'd have to start reading the Sunday society page, he supposed. As if he didn't have enough to worry about.

Rosalind seemed to sense a chink in his armor. Her face took on a certain crafty gleam. "That came from Nadine's final column before she sailed off into the sunset on that cruise she won—praise the Lord. You want it to appear in the *Bandwagon*?"

"Not like that, which is why I hire editors—to make it better."

"You think that's possible? If you had to read this stuff every week, you'd know what we go through out there in the newsroom."

She shuffled the pages and pulled out another. "Okay, let's try this one—'Palpitating with some pristine and palatable pleasures, the beautifully extravagant night held out its velvety arms to offer a respite from the shabby oblivion of the daily grind.' " She looked up. "Would you believe this is a story about a potluck dinner?"

Nick stared at her, both intrigued and appalled by such misuse of the language. The newspaper had gone through a half-dozen social columnists in as many months. Some had quit in despair; some had been fired; some had found urgent business elsewhere when their inadequacies became glaring.

Nadine had been hired with high hopes that she would be the one to fill the shoes of the popular *Bandwagon* columnist Mildred Higgenbotham. Millie, as her friends called her, had been head librarian and social arbiter of their sunny Southern California community. When she retired and moved to Rocky Comfort, Missouri, the town of Buena Vista had practically gone into mourning.

Nick knew Millie was a hard act to follow but this was ridiculous. "I'll admit that's not very good," he conceded, trying to soothe his incensed editor, "but you and Debbie are pros. You can work with anyone. With a little guidance..."

Roz gave an indignant sniff. "Okay," she snapped, "I didn't want to resort to this but you've forced my hand." She extracted a strip of waxed type from between the pages. "And don't blame Debbie—she's been working like a horse, covering for vacations and all. When editors get exhausted stuff slips past." She began to read:

"'Convinced of their propelling potency, the Clover Valley United Church Women put on a homemade guacamole fund-raiser and emerged covered with glorious resplendency in their enterprising undertaking.'"

Nick gave her a bland smile. "Hey, not bad," he said, stretching the point by at least a mile. "A little judicious editing and we're all set."

"I am not finished," Rosalind stated ruthlessly. "To continue... 'The benefit was to benefit Gregory Atkinson, whose lifelong aspiration is to facilitate as a missionary in some Third World country.'"

"So?" Nick raised his brows.

"'While the seminarian prepared for the missionary position, his wife, the lovely Louisa, is also anticipating life stretched out in service.'"

Nick slumped back in his chair, tasting defeat. "Stop! Show a little mercy." He held out his hands, a gesture of compromise. "Nadine's already quit. So hire somebody, already."

Roz gave him an evil smile. "Aw, come on. Don't you want to hear about how the real homemade guacamole made out of real olive-green avocados brought tears of childish memories to the throngs of assorted dignitaries and high-muck-a-mucks?''

He sank deeper into his chair. ''I don't know how you developed that mean streak,'' he complained.

''Dealing with Nadine and others of her ilk.''

''Then run right out and hire someone better. But not Annie Page.''

''Be reasonable, Nick. Annie's a natural. Everybody likes her—''

''I don't.''

''—and respects her. She's a volunteer for every worthy organization in town—''

''Anyone but her.''

''—and she's got more contacts than you and me put together.''

''How about Myrna Fairchild?''

''Married a butcher and moved to Phoenix. About Annie—she's actually a literate woman. She listens when you talk to her. Do you have any idea how exciting that is? We could *teach* her. She's capable of *learning*.''

''No, damn it! Don't you understand what 'no' means?''

She cocked her head to one side, her annoyance manifest. With her curly red hair and animated manner, she reminded Nick of a chrysanthemum. Annie Page, on the other hand, made him think of a lily...all smooth creamy skin, pale expressionless face and waxen personality.

He respected a fighter like Roz. He neither liked nor trusted those who, like Annie, kept a tight rein on their emotions. She was too perfect, and perfection was as unnatural as...as red cabbage or purple roses.

But then, Roz was a woman. Mrs. Page was a *lady*.

"Tell me the real reason," Roz pressed. "What have you got against Annie, besides her choice in husbands?"

"Isn't that enough?" He leaned forward and picked up the small, primitive sculpture of some obscure Indian god, given to him by a Central American guerrilla. It was the only nonfunctional item on his desk. He turned the rough stone representation over and over in his hands. He'd always preferred substance to style.

Roz glared at him. "No, it's not enough," she said with the tenacity of the born journalist.

"Then try this—Annie Page is a goody-two-shoes, a phony-baloney Lady Bountiful who never had a thought in her head that wasn't put there by her husband."

Rosalind pursed her lips. "You've said that so often I think you actually believe it. Boy, you are so wrong!"

He shrugged. "She's not called the 'society Page' for nothing."

"That's a—" Her hot words broke off and she brightened. "That's a great name for her column. Umm, the 'Society Page.' It's also a quick and easy way to let the town know you two have buried the hatchet."

As if we could, Nick thought. He set the memento of his traveling days on his desk, stood up and walked to the window. *Could either of us ever get past the political rivalry between this newspaper and the late Mayor Robert Page?*

The final blow-up between Nick and Mayor Page had occurred slightly more than a year ago, just days before the mayor was stricken with the heart attack that ultimately killed him. Page, a no-growth advocate, was adamantly opposed to a new city recreation center that had been highly touted in the pages of the *Bandwagon*.

Nick's editorials had swayed public opinion and carried the day; the new recreation center would open later this summer. The irate mayor—a bad loser as always—had vowed never to set foot inside the building. He also vowed never to allow another issue of the Buena Vista *Bandwagon* inside his home on Avocado Avenue, the ritziest residential area in town.

His wife, the "society Page" in Nick's scornful lexicon, had stood there with an insipid smile on her face while the "political Page" delivered this asinine ultimatum. Nick couldn't imagine what it would take to get a show of honest emotion out of her, but he was positive it would be a lot more than a part-time job at the newspaper despised by her husband.

"Hey, you in there?"

Nick blinked back to the present. "Sorry. I was thinking."

"Obviously. So what about Annie? Shall I call her or do you want to do it?"

"Give it up, Roz." He hesitated. "She wouldn't work here anyway," he predicted. "Sure, she's got the contacts, but she's too much of a society snob to hold a real job. It'd be beneath her dignity."

Roz resorted to wheedling. "If she says 'no,' I'll quit nagging you about it and look somewhere else. But can we at least ask?"

"Damn it, Rosalind, you're turning into a royal pain in the—"

"Neck—I know. And I know something else. Annie's going to be named the Buena Vista Citizen of the Year next month at the Chamber of Commerce awards dinner. And you'll have to make the presentation, since the paper always pays for the trophy." She gave him an anxious glance. "This is top secret, you understand."

"I know how to keep a secret," Nick muttered. "But I can't imagine it—me, standing up there in front of God and everybody, saying nice things about Annie Page. Kind of boggles the mind. I wouldn't be surprised if old Mayor Page turned over in his grave.'' He grinned.

"That possibility troubles you, I can see.'' Roz's tone was dry. "Take it to its ultimate conclusion—put her on the payroll. Think of all that would accomplish . . . you'd make my life a lot easier, improve the quality of this newspaper beyond measure and throw the entire city of Buena Vista into a frenzy of speculation. Offer her the job, Nick.''

Nick stroked his thick dark mustache as he considered. Things had been dull lately, he admitted to himself. In some ways, he rather missed Mayor Page, who'd always been good for a headline, an editorial or a fight.

Then, in his mind's eye, he saw the prim and prissy Mrs. Page, smiling serenely as she walked into a lion's den.

He snorted and shook his head. *She'll never do it.* "A snowball's got a better chance of surviving in hell than we do of getting Annie Page to work at this newspaper,'' he prophesied.

"Is that a yes? I think I hear a yes!'' An expression of gleeful satisfaction settled across Roz's freckled face. "She's as good as hired. Because you, Nicholas Madison Kimball, are the most determined man I've ever met.''

Her eyes flicked to the sign above his desk. He didn't have to turn his head to know its message—*The name of the game is perseverance.*

Roz stood up. "The hard part was getting you to admit you want her,'' she said, her voice heavy with satisfaction.

Want Annie Page? Not likely, Nick thought. But in the interests of peace, he conceded a minor point. "Okay, if I happen to run into her around town, I might bring it up. Now will you get out of here and let me go back to work?''

Rosalind tossed her handful of papers onto his desk. "Just in case you weaken," she said as she turned away.

Nick waited until the door closed behind her before picking up a badly typed sheet. "'The brawny, macho, madcap "boys" of Buena Vista put together many a powerhouse enterprise with allegiant endeavors to magnify its philanthropic projects,'" he read. "'Those passionate about their tummies recently were aflutter to find edibles on a half shell of gargantuan proportion—'"

Nick dropped the paper and groaned. Annie Page might not be such a bad idea after all. He didn't think she'd ever been passionate about anything, and certainly not about tummies.

CHAPTER ONE

ANNIE TURNED HER HEAD quickly, letting her dark shoulder-length hair swing across the side of her face to hide her sudden tears. For a moment she couldn't bring herself to respond to George Drinker's offer for the eight beautiful satinwood Hepplewhite chairs.

It wasn't enough. It wasn't nearly enough, and yet she knew Mr. Drinker wouldn't cheat her. He'd been coming to her home for months now to look over the family heirlooms whose sale had kept her financially afloat. He'd given her a good price on the chiffonier the last time, and on the sideboard the time before that. But she'd thought . . . hoped . . . prayed the chairs would bring more.

"You all right, Mrs. Page?"

She heard the concern in his voice and felt a stab of guilt. None of this was his fault, of course. She swallowed hard and took a deep breath, turning her head to look at him. She tried to make her smile convincing.

"I'm fine, Mr. Drinker." She touched the oval back of one chair, lightly tracing the inlaid flower motif with her fingertips. *It's only furniture,* she reminded herself. *Grandmother would understand.*

The burly antiques dealer shifted uncomfortably, a frown creasing his chubby face. "Hey, well now, I could go a couple of hundred higher," he said in a too-hearty voice. "Wouldn't want to cheat one of my best customers."

Annie winced, and he seemed to realize his words had hardly comforted her. He patted her arm with a clumsy hand. "Hey, well now," he said, "I oughta learn to keep my big mouth shut. I didn't mean—"

"It's all right, really it is. I accept your offer." She gave him a shaky grin. "Your *first* offer which I'm sure was more than fair."

"Ah, Mrs. Page..." He shuffled from one foot to the other and dipped his head, looking vastly uncomfortable.

She spoke more briskly, now that the shock was fading. "I didn't hesitate because I distrusted you, Mr. Drinker. I hesitated because of all the memories tied up in these sticks of wood."

He nodded. "Yeah, well now, I know what you mean. If you'd like to change your mind..."

She shook her head with great conviction. "Heavens, no! I'm redecorating and they wouldn't fit in at all." The lie did not come easily, but it did come.

"In that case," he said, moving toward the hallway, "I'll take 'em with pleasure. Can I send the truck by this afternoon, Mrs. Page?"

"By all means, Mr. Drinker."

She followed him outside and watched as he pointed his pickup down the curving driveway in front of her home, past the slender palm trees and the bank of azalea bushes. When he was out of sight, she carefully and quietly closed the front door, walked through the silent house and entered the big master bedroom.

For a few moments she stood stiffly in the middle of the room, looking around her, feeling as bland as the clean white walls. There were only two pieces of furniture left in there: a small chest of drawers with a mirror, and a king-size bed where she slept alone each night.

And where she cried alone, when it all became too much.

The telephone on the floor let out a piercing ring that jolted her. Moving with jerky steps, she crossed the room and snatched it up. She slumped on the bed and placed the phone beside her on the plain white spread before lifting the receiver.

"Hello?" Her voice cracked; she swallowed hard and repeated the greeting.

There was a moment's silence, and then Lew asked, "Mom? Annie, is that you?"

The sound of her stepson's voice steadied her as nothing else could. She sat up straighter. "Hi, honey."

"You sound funny. Is anything wrong?"

She thought fast. "A summer cold. You know how hard they are to shake. I'm okay—tell me about you. The cast driving you crazy?"

He uttered a dramatic groan. "Wish I'd broken my arm instead of my leg. Then there'd be no point in summer classes, right?"

"Wrong."

They both laughed, but Annie knew that Lew was serious about his studies. He was in college by choice, not because he'd been pushed there by an overzealous parent. When Robert had tried, Lew rebelled. He'd bummed around on his own for the year following high school graduation before finally admitting Father really did know best—Lew needed that college education. He returned home at nineteen, only a few months before Robert's death.

Annie was the only mother Lew had ever known. It was she who'd struggled to keep father and son from each other's throats during Lew's "terrible teens," she who'd rejoiced when they found their way back to that special father-son relationship. Although Robert was dead, Lew, only fifteen years her junior was still her son and always would be.

"Yes, Mommy," he teased now. "I'll study hard and uphold the family honor. That'll be an easy promise to keep, under the circumstances. Until this cast comes off, studying's about the only thing I *can* do."

Annie's heart went out to her son, normally so active. "Does it hurt much?" she asked.

"Only when I laugh," he said, laughing. "The reason I called, Mom—"

"You need a reason these days?"

"Trying to watch the old phone bill. The thing is, there seems to be some mix-up in my tuition for this summer session." He hesitated. "Mom, is there some problem? If there is, just say so. I can still withdraw until September and look for a summer job."

She squeezed her eyes tightly closed and grasped the receiver so hard her fingers whitened. After a moment, she opened her eyes, relaxed her muscles and said in a perfectly normal voice, "That's a swell idea. Must be lots of jobs out there for guys with one leg in a cast."

"I mean it," he insisted. "I feel like a freeloader as it is. If we're having some kind of temporary cash flow problem—"

"Stop, Lew! I've been busy, that's all. Don't you remember how I am when I try to do too much? I'll get the check in the mail by the end of the week."

He let out his breath in an explosive sigh and she knew he'd accepted her explanation.

"That's a relief," he admitted. "I was afraid something was wrong."

"How many times do I have to tell you, honey? I'm the parent. It's my job to worry. You're the kid. It's your job to study hard and get a good education so you can take care of me in my old age.''

They laughed together, and the conversation turned to trivial matters. Somehow Annie managed to keep her anxiety at bay, but after they'd hung up, she sat for a long time on the bed, staring at nothing.

Counting what she'd get for the chairs, she'd have the money for Lew's summer tuition and maybe enough left over to call a plumber to fix the leaking faucets in the hall bathroom and the kitchen. But if anything else broke down or wore out, it'd be all over... and something always did.

Then there was the Kids' Club's annual fund drive. Every year the Pages had given $250. At the moment, that might as well be $250,000.

She'd kept all this from Lew. He hadn't been home since Christmas, when the decorated tree had gone a long way toward disguising a certain bare quality to the living room. Now there was nothing left to fill the blank spots where furniture used to be. He'd take one look and know.

She'd protect him as long as she could, though. Lucky for her, he wasn't an extravagant kid. He'd carried a full load of classes during his just-finished freshman year, and held down a job as well. Because he started college a year behind his contemporaries, he'd stayed on for the summer session to make up for lost time. His part-time campus employment had handled most of his day-to-day expenses, until the accident.

But now I've got to level with him, Annie admitted, leaning over to replace the telephone on the floor beside the bed. Lew, like everyone else, thought Robert had provided generously for his widow and his son. Lew didn't know that bad investments and poor planning had caught up with his father.

Annie hadn't known either, until it was too late. "Women shouldn't have to worry about such matters," Robert often said. How she wished she'd argued that point. When he died, she hadn't even known where to find his insurance policy.

She'd learned, but many of the lessons were expensive ones. Now, despite her best efforts, she dangled from the end of her financial rope. Something had to be done, and quickly.

For the first time in her thirty-five years, she was going to have to find herself a paying job.

And Annie Page was scared.

ANNIE FIXED HERSELF a glass of iced tea, tucked a yellow legal pad beneath one arm, grabbed a pencil and carried everything out onto the redwood deck at the back of the house. Might as well enjoy the view while she still had it, she told herself, setting her supplies on a small wooden table. She sank into a padded lounge chair beneath a leafy canopy of pepper trees and looked around as if seeing all the beauty for the first time.

The deck faced west, clinging to a hill on the eastern edge of the city. The view was breathtaking, with the Pacific shimmering miles away in brilliant golden sunlight.

She'd tried to talk Robert out of buying the house, since both homes and lots on Avocado Drive were much too big and expensive. As always, he'd prevailed. She had to admit she'd enjoyed living there, at least when she'd been able to afford the upkeep.

She'd have to put the place on the market soon. She had no choice, really, as much as she dreaded losing her home, risking the pity of the community or making some disastrous financial mistake. That frightened her most of all— fear of making the wrong choices.

That was why she'd procrastinated . . . that and the possibility of damaging Robert's standing in the community, should it become known that he'd left his family in dire financial straits. Robert had guarded his reputation all his life; now it was up to her to do it for him.

But Lew's fall tuition had to come from somewhere. She had to do something, even if she did it wrong.

She picked up the pad and pencil, determined not to be sidetracked. At the top of the page, she wrote in large block letters the word *JOB*.

Beneath it, she wrote Pros on one side and Cons on the other. Then she stared at the sheet of paper. And stared.

Finally under Pros she wrote, "I know a lot of people." That was true. But was that a pro or a con? After a few minutes of contemplation, she marked out that first entry with dark determined strokes and turned to the Con list.

Setting her jaw, she wrote rapidly:

1) I have no talent, no experience and no one will ever hire me.

2) If by some miracle I find a job, I won't get any kind of salary because no one in town will believe I need the money.

3) If anyone does figure out I need the money, they'll think Robert was a bad provider.

She hesitated. After a moment's deliberation she crossed out *"was a bad provider"* and inserted *"wasn't as good a provider as they believed."* After more thought, she continued her list.

4) If Lew finds out, he'll feel guilty and drop out of school.

Anything but that, she thought, chewing on the eraser. She'd dropped out of college herself because of guilt, not guilt over money but over shirking family responsibilities.

"Family loyalty comes first, Annie," her father had ground into her consciousness. "I know you won't let me down. You can always go to college later, but right now your mother needs you. If her 'problem' becomes public knowledge..."

Her mother's problem was alcohol; her father's problem was making sure no one outside the family suspected. Zealously he guarded his reputation as an up-and-coming career Army officer, drawing his daughter into the conspiracy to deny his wife's addiction.

It hadn't been easy for him. It hadn't been easy for Annie, either. But loyalty had been born and bred into her very soul and she didn't have to be coaxed to do the right thing, no matter how difficult that might be.

But she couldn't avoid an occasional regret. She'd never had an opportunity to return to college and she rued that fact to this day. If it took her last penny, she'd see that her stepson completed his education.

With a sigh, she slumped back in her chair and closed her eyes to ward off melancholy thoughts. As she relaxed, she became aware of the song of birds and the rustle of a breeze in the treetops. She opened her eyes, just as a butterfly wafted past. Its blue and green wings shimmered like silk.

"The best things in life really are free," she said out loud. She picked up her pad again and under the Pro column, wrote in big black letters: "NECESSITY."

DECIDING TO FIND a job was one thing; finding it was something else again. The logical place to start would be with the Help Wanted advertisements in the newspaper, she supposed. That presented a problem, since there hadn't been a copy of the Buena Vista *Bandwagon* in the house since Robert nearly came to blows with the publisher, Nicholas Kimball.

Annie didn't know Mr. Kimball personally, but she certainly knew him from the pages of the newspaper Robert routinely referred to as "that rag." The *Bandwagon*'s unfounded and scurrilous attacks on Robert had caused Annie untold grief. Since her husband's death, she had tried valiantly to uphold his standards and beliefs, which including shunning the newspaper.

But desperate times called for desperate measures. By the time she walked into the board meeting of the Buena Vista Kids' Club the next morning, Annie was desperate, all right.

As usual, there were several copies of the *Bandwagon* strewn around the room. They tantalized her through the entire meeting.

At its conclusion, board members straggled out while Annie pretended great interest in organizing her portfolio. When she was finally alone in the conference room, she snatched up a copy of the newspaper. She resisted an urge to simply stuff it inside her portfolio and walk out; that would be stealing. Trying to calm her jangled nerves, she turned to the classified ads.

Quickly she perused the opportunities available for certified apartment managers (no—that required a couple), construction foam installers, auto salespeople, carpenters, child care workers, cosmetic salespeople, delivery drivers, dental assistants, exotic dancers, hairdressers, mechanic/installers—

Outside the door, she heard the voice of Mike Andrews, executive director of the club. Her fingers tightened convulsively on the newsprint, wrinkling the pages—

there must be something! I'm not ready for exotic danc-ing and that's the most promising thing I've found.

Salesperson! Her eyes zeroed in on the listing. At the Buena Vista Fine Apparel Shop for Men and Women— Larry Rayburn's store. She and Larry served together on the board of directors of the Buena Vista Cultural Foundation.

Could she approach him? Would it be harder to ask a stranger or a friend for employment? Maybe she could—

"You still here?"

Mike stood in the doorway, grinning. She felt her face flush and she dropped the incriminating newspaper. "I was—I just thought I'd—I didn't—"

"Hey, take it easy." He gave her a curious glance and walked to his place at the head of the conference table. "There's nothing wrong with reading the local paper, Annie. Thousands of people do it every day."

She shrugged, unable to meet his eyes. "To each his own," she said coolly. "I gave in to idle curiosity. That's the first copy I've looked at since Robert cancelled our subscription."

Mike picked up the reports lying on the table. "I'm sorry to hear that," he replied. "It was bad enough, two of the most prominent men in town fighting like little boys, but I thought you had more sense than to perpetuate the feud."

His tone was indulgent, but his words offended her anyway. As if Robert shared the blame, she thought indignantly. Nicholas Kimball had been totally at fault for the feud—totally!

"I'm not perpetuating a thing," she said with a smile designed to conceal her true feelings. She tucked her hair smoothly and severely behind her ears and reached for her purse and portfolio.

"Aren't you?"

His question brought her head swinging up and a puzzled frown to her face. "What do you mean, Mike?"

"I mean, if it's over, there's no reason you shouldn't read the *Bandwagon* like the rest of the town."

He strode around the table, picked up the paper and tucked it beneath her arm. Then he grinned as if he'd done something brilliant. "Read it in good health," he invited.

She was too embarrassed to argue. With a noncommittal smile, she walked out of the conference room, out of the club and straight to the trash barrel beside the front door.

She felt enormously better, once she'd deposited the *Bandwagon* where it belonged.

The drive downtown took only five minutes. She pulled into a parking lot and turned off the engine... and sat there, clutching the steering wheel with clammy hands. She couldn't seem to work up enough nerve to get out of the car, she realized with self-loathing.

She'd never dreamed it could be so hard to ask for a job. Did everybody go through this? Surely not—if they did, the unemployment rate would skyrocket.

Not that she'd never wanted a job. As a teen she'd begged her father to let her work during the summer vacations but he wouldn't even discuss it. "You know your mother needs you," the colonel had said. "How can you even ask?"

So she'd quit asking. But then, a few years after her marriage, Annie had lucked into an opportunity to work part-time at her favorite bookstore. When she went to Robert with the exciting news, she'd read the disappointment in his eyes.

"If that's what's important to you, by all means go ahead," he'd said. "Of course, it'll be hard on Lew, but he's been without a mother before—he'll survive. I suppose we can entertain less. That probably won't hurt my career *too* much."

Even in retrospect, she couldn't blame him for taking that attitude, she acknowledged as she forced herself to climb out of the car. *Everything he said was true. It would have been incredibly selfish of me to take a job then. But now everything's different.*

Yes, different. Now nobody was offering her anything, and over the years, she'd forgotten how to ask…if she ever knew.

At the door of the Buena Vista Fine Apparel Shop for Men and Women, she drew a deep determined breath. Then, throat dry and hands damp, she walked inside.

"May I help you?"

A salesclerk's voice made Annie jump with surprise. "N-no. I'm just looking."

The gray-haired woman smiled. "Take your time. If I can be of any assistance, please ask."

The woman moved away, pausing nearby to adjust garments hanging on a rack. *Ask her,* Annie ordered herself. *Ask her!*

"Uhhh…ma'am?"

The salesclerk glanced up from her task. "Yes?"

"Is…is Larry…is Mr. Rayburn in?"

The woman craned her neck toward the back of the store. "He's on the telephone. May I tell him who's here?"

"Oh, no, no, please don't bother him." Annie took a hasty step back and bumped into a display of men's sport coats. "If I'm still shopping when he's finished, I'll just say hello."

"As you like," the woman said. She drifted off, straightening clothing as she went.

Annie eased toward the door, hoping Larry hadn't caught sight of her. That was a close call, she thought, preparing to flee. *I've got to get out of here and rethink this situation. I'll just go on back home and—*

She stopped short, her eyes widening. In the doorway, between her and a clean getaway, stood Nicholas Kimball, her sworn enemy. Talk about being between the devil and the deep blue sea, she groaned inwardly.

She swerved aside and slipped behind a tall rack of dresses. She didn't think he'd seen her; from her hiding place, she watched him step inside and turn toward a display of shirts.

He was bigger than she remembered, more than six feet tall, and some women might find him good-looking despite the mustache—Robert *despised* mustaches. She'd never had the opportunity, or the desire, to study Mr. Kimball this way. She took advantage of it now with a vague and unformed hoped that she could somehow fathom what made him so wrong-minded in his dealings with Robert.

Nick Kimball wore casual clothing, in keeping with the Southern California life-style, but the navy trousers and pale blue cotton pullover had an expensive look to them. Or maybe anything he wore would look good, Annie considered as she appraised his wide-shouldered, narrow-hipped body.

He turned slightly and spoke to the salesclerk, who hurried to his side. Annie scrutinized his strong profile, more dismayed by the moment. What a shame, that someone so vindictive and misguided should be so...would it be disloyal to use the word *handsome* to describe him?

As she debated the moral issue, he looked around, the movement of his head so sudden and unexpected that she had no time to react. His alert blue gaze slammed into her with an almost physical impact; she took a step backward and smashed into something—someone who let out a soft "Oomph!"

She felt hands on her arms, steadying her, and looked wildly over her shoulder and into the surprised and fatherly face of Larry Rayburn.

"Easy there, little lady," he chuckled. "Didn't mean to scare you that way."

"You didn't. I mean—" Better to let him think so. "That's all right. I wasn't paying attention. Did I step on your foot?"

"Yes, but I don't think it's broken." He gave her shoulder a friendly squeeze before releasing her. "You haven't been around here for a while. Looking for something special or did you just drop in to say hi?"

She hadn't been in because she hadn't spent a penny on clothing for herself in at least six months, but of course she didn't say that. "I'm not looking for anything special, just targets of opportunity," she fudged. *Oh dear! I must sound like a fool—"targets of opportunity," indeed!*

"Got time for a cup of coffee?"

"Wh-why..." Why not? Maybe the conversation would turn in some direction that would give her an opening: *By the way, I understand you're looking for a salesclerk and it just so happens I'm looking for a job.* "I'd love a cup of coffee," she said.

"Good." He patted her arm. "Why don't you go on back and help yourself while I say hello to Nick. I'll be right with you."

Her heart sank, but she nodded and turned to do as he suggested. Just when she'd thought things couldn't get any worse, Nicholas Kimball had to show up, she thought unhappily. If he joined them for coffee....

But Mr. Kimball didn't join them for coffee, thank heavens. Only Larry made his way to the back of the store a few minutes later. She finished pouring the coffee and handed him a cup, adding cream and sugar to her own.

"So," he said, pausing to take a sip, "what have you been up to? Keeping busy?"

Aha! An opening, she thought. "Well, actually, I seem to have a lot of extra time on my hands these days." She stared into her cup as if it held the answer to life's mysteries.

He nodded wisely, his eyes understanding behind the wire-framed glasses. "I remember how it was when my wife died. Hard. Real hard." He took a sip of coffee. "I was lucky I had this place to keep me busy until I found Linda—or she found me."

"Yes. Uhh...I..." *Go on, say the rest. Ask him for the job.* She swallowed hard and licked her lips. "I wish I had something like that to keep me busy. I—"

The salesclerk's voice cut across Annie's hesitant words. "Excuse me—Larry, Nick's interested in the new polos in red. I thought maybe that Monday shipment..."

"Sorry, that's all summer stuff. We won't have anything in red for at least another month."

The nape of Annie's neck prickled, and she sensed that Mr. Kimball had approached. She kept her gaze lowered, trying to use the interruption to get a grip on herself. After a few more comments on available colors, Larry shifted in his chair.

"Sorry," he said to Annie. "I've been filling in around here as everything from stock boy to bookkeeper. If I don't get some help soon, Linda's going to give me my walking papers."

So what are you waiting for? she scolded herself. *An engraved invitation?* "We wouldn't want that," she replied, trying to sound confident. "Maybe I could give you a hand."

Annie couldn't believe she'd said that; obviously Larry was as astounded as she, for he stared at her with mouth agape.

"Now there's a thought," he said finally. "I could probably use a fine volunteer like you, but what I really need is somebody who's ambitious and wants to learn retail."

"Oh." Deflated, Annie sank back in her chair. She wasn't ambitious, and although she found retail mildly interesting, she wasn't looking for a profession. She was simply looking for a way to pay a few overdue bills. "I just thought maybe...I mean, if you really need someone...I'm a fast learner and..."

"Annie, Annie, Annie." Larry leaned forward and patted her hand. "You are just about the nicest person I know. Imagine that! Not only do you give your time and talents unselfishly to every worthy cause in town, now you're even willing to pitch in to help a friend."

"I'm not exactly ready for sainthood," Annie objected. "I just thought... I mean, if you'd feel better paying me..." Her heart leaped. *Maybe this will work out after all. Oh, please let him say yes!*

He didn't say yes. He chuckled again, not in a malicious way, but it hurt her just the same.

"Dear girl, you really are lonely, aren't you? Tell you what I'm going to do—I'm going to have my sister-in-law give you a call. You know Ruby, don't you? She's in this singles group and they have such good times."

As he talked, Annie's cheeks burned hotter and hotter. She didn't know which was worse, the truth or letting him believe she was lonely enough to join a singles club.

She lifted her cup to her lips and in so doing, raised her eyes. Nicholas Kimball stood not ten feet away, his face alight with curiosity. Their gazes touched for just an in stant, and he tipped his head gravely in her direction. She nodded without smiling and looked away, startled and disconcerted by the sudden acceleration of the pulse pounding in her throat.

Larry was winding down. "So you see, although I appreciate your gesture, it wouldn't be right to take bread out of the mouths of people who need it, just to give you something to do." He looked at her expectantly.

She put her cup on the table and stood up. "You're absolutely right, Larry. Now that I think about it, I'm not really going to have that much extra time this summer after all." She glanced around, just in time to see Mr. Kimball walk out the front door. Relief washed over her. "I've about decided to put the house on the market and you know how much time and bother that will be," she concluded more confidently.

Larry followed her through the store. "I'll bet you're going to move to Thunder Valley," he guessed, naming Buena Vista's newest housing development. "Nice homes—you can get in for less than $250,000, I hear."

Annie, who would have had trouble coming up with 250,000 beans, nodded. "So I hear." She paused at the door. "Thanks for the coffee, Larry. I'll see you Thursday at the Cultural Foundation board meeting."

"See you Thursday."

He opened the door for her and she stepped through. As the door closed behind her, her shoulders sagged. What an unmitigated, unholy, unbelievable fiasco! After that, her day had nowhere to go but up.

Or so she thought. A shadow fell across her path and Nicholas Kimball stepped in front of her, barring her way.

She stopped short, intimidated by his height and the breadth of his shoulders.

"Well, what do you know," he said, his silky tone immediately arousing her suspicions. "It's Annie Page. I promised somebody that the next time I ran into you, I'd offer you a cup of coffee and a glamorous career in journalism. Interested?"

CHAPTER TWO

WAS ANNIE INTERESTED in anything that required her to spend time in that man's company? "Not even a little bit, Mr. Kimball," she said, speaking with uncharacteristic frankness because he'd caught her off guard. "Good day."

Eager to escape his intimidating presence, she marched away, heading toward the lot where she'd parked her six-year-old Chevrolet. She felt a trifle guilty about being so ungracious, but he made her much too nervous to engage in polite chitchat. She'd never been comfortable around the man, and her husband's death had apparently made the situation worse, not better.

"Nick. Call me Nick. And I'll call you Annie."

He fell into step beside her, on the outside, she noticed. Robert had always walked on the outside, next to traffic or possible danger, an old-fashioned courtesy that made her feel protected and cherished.

Usually made her feel protected and cherished, she amended, giving her companion a wide berth. Everything about Nicholas Kimball made her feel threatened and insecure.

"Mr. Kimball, I really am in a hurry."

"Nick, remember?"

He smiled and the creases in his lean cheeks deepened. Annie halted beside her car, refusing to be charmed by him.

"All right," she conceded. "Nick." She looked past his shoulder, mystified by his persistence. In all the time they'd known each other, they'd never had a private conversation. Why was he doing this now? she wondered. "It's kind of you to ask but I really must decline." She opened her purse and searched around for the car key.

He frowned, whether in disappointment or irritation she couldn't imagine.

"It's not kind of me to ask," he corrected. "Kind doesn't enter into it—I'm never kind, ask anybody. Believe me, if I hadn't promised—" He broke off abruptly. "Never mind that. I really do have something important to discuss with you. Jut a few minutes of your time, that's all I require."

She shook her head stubbornly. "We have nothing to say to each other, now or ever. You'll have to excuse me."

She unlocked the car door, studiously avoiding his eyes. She could feel his anger and that was enough; she didn't want to confront or acknowledge it further.

She started to swing the door open, but he reached out and held it closed. "Look, lady," he began. "I don't want to get—"

"Annie!"

The voice calling her name distracted them both. Glancing across the parking lot, she saw an elderly woman in a wheelchair. A young man propelled the chair forward while the woman waved and called out enthusiastically.

"Oh, dear," Annie said beneath her breath. It was Mrs. Kopeckne, and the young man pushing the wheelchair must be her grandson, the one of whom she spoke with such boundless enthusiasm.

Nick's hand fell away from the door and Annie pulled it open without interference. *I could just wave, jump in the car and leave,* she thought wistfully—but she wouldn't.

Crotchety old Mrs. Kopeckne's pride was too easily offended, and she had few enough friends as it was.

The wheelchair bounced over the pebbly parking lot and came to a halt beside the car, the elderly passenger breathing as hard as if she'd done the pushing. She twisted sideways and grasped the young man's hand.

"This is my grandson, William," she said eagerly. Her expression, normally reminiscent of one eating unripe persimmons, was radiant. "Billy, this is Mr. Kimball, who works at the newspaper, and my special friend, Annie Page."

Annie reached out to shake Billy's hand. "Hi. Your grandmother and I spend a lot of time together at the Senior Citizens' Center."

"Yeah, hi," Billy mumbled. He looked uncomfortable. His glance swung past her and halted on Nick.

Nick stuck out his hand. His entire manner had changed and he seemed alert and watchful. His eyes narrowed as he looked at the boy. "Don't I know you from somewhere?" he asked in a wary tone.

The kid shifted from one foot to the other. "Nah." He released Nick's hand as if it burned him. "We better go, Grandma. Gotta get you back by lunchtime."

Mrs. Kopeckne beamed. "He's such a good boy," she confided. "Annie, will I see you tomorrow at the Senior Center? You promised to bind off that afghan for me. Remember?"

"I remember, Mrs. Kopeckne. You can count on me."

Annie watched Billy wheel his grandmother away. When they were out of sight behind a row of cars, she couldn't resist turning toward Nick.

"What was that all about?"

"Nothing."

"That sounds suspiciously like 'something.'"

"Intuitive little thing, aren't you. The name sounded familiar, that's all." He lounged against the car door, holding it open but not wide enough for her to enter. "William Kopeckne...I probably read it in the paper. I hope it was in connection with 4-H or high school sports, not the police blotter."

Annie felt her hackles rise. Some people never seemed to grasp the concept of "innocent until proven guilty." She didn't envy Nick, going through life always expecting the worst of people. "Billy seems like a very nice young man to me," she said defensively. "At least his grandmother loves him."

Nick's eyebrows rose and his blue eyes took on a devilish glint. His mouth curved in a wicked-looking grin. "I had a grandmother who thought *I* was a very nice young man, once upon a time. Is that a strong enough reference to get you into Hoffy's for a cup of coffee with me?"

Surprisingly enough, it took all her strength of will not to grin back at him. There was something infectious about his smile that she'd never noticed before. She knew she should be immune to the inherent charm of the man, but his lopsided grin threatened to push preconceived notions right out of her mind.

She stiffened her spine. It would take more than charm to make Annie Page forget her priorities. She opened her mouth to refuse—courteously, of course.

He waited with such an avid expression that all of a sudden she realized he *expected* her to turn him down. If she did, he'd try a new approach, but he wouldn't give up. Here was a man who just plain loved a challenge.

Her lips thinned disapprovingly. "I suppose stubborn determination is considered a virtue in your line of work."

He braced his arms on top of the car door and leaned closer. "In Joe Public, it's stubbornness. In Joe Journalist, it's perseverance, and a highly valued commodity."

"Whatever you call it, I—"

He silenced her with an upheld hand. "Let me save us both some time," he suggested. "I'm not going to give up until you listen to me. I always get my way, so if you're smart you'll give in gracefully."

She bit off the hot words of denial that trembled on her lips. How did this man manage to make her consistently forget her manners? No wonder Robert found him impossible!

"Yes?" he urged, a smile hovering around his lips.

She gave an exasperated sigh. "I suddenly find myself resigned to hearing what you have to say. But no coffee. You can talk right here."

He glanced at his wristwatch, a heavy gold timepiece she was sure had Rolex stamped on it somewhere. "Sorry," he said, not sounding sorry in the least. He took her elbow in a firm grip and steered her toward the sidewalk. "You've argued so long it's lunchtime. On the *Bandwagon*, of course—the best the coffee shop has to offer. Sky's the limit. Try the steak sandwich and fries, anything at all. Live dangerously."

She felt as if she were. Although he hurried her along, she couldn't miss the astonished stares of people they passed. Mrs. Steinberger, sweeping off the sidewalk in front of Steinberger's Drug Emporium, actually dropped her broom and gaped.

Nick gave the woman a friendly hello and Annie offered a strained smile; there wasn't time for more. His fingers burned her arm but she submitted to his touch, rather than risk a scene. She was breathless by the time they reached their destination.

Nick swept open the door of Hoffy's Coffee Shop with a flourish. Watching him, Annie could well understand how Sir Walter Raleigh might have dazzled Queen Elizabeth I with that cloak-over-the-mud-puddle stunt. Nick was the same kind of swashbuckler, but he might also be the kind who'd pull the rug—or the cloak—out from under an unwary foot. Hadn't he withdrawn his editorial support from Robert at the last minute?

Flustered by Nick's audacity, she led the way inside. Now that he no longer touched her, she felt her equilibrium returning. As they waited for the hostess to seat them, she paused and looked around, determined to appear calm and in control.

And wished she hadn't. She must have known at least half of the people crowding the little restaurant. Every one of them seemed to be looking at her, and she was sure they were all wondering why the mayor's widow was walking in with his worst enemy, bold as brass.

The waitress snatched up a menu and approached, a broad grin on her face. She glanced past Annie and apparently saw Nick for her eyes widened. "Hi ya, Annie," she said. "One for lunch?"

Nick's hand closed over Annie's elbow again as if he owned it. "Make that two for lunch, Connie," he instructed. "The lady's my guest."

Connie's jaw dropped. "You're kidding!"

Annie could have died of embarrassment. If there was anything she hated, it was being the focus of public curiosity. And the increased pressure of Nick's fingers on her bare arm didn't help matters.

The waitress pulled herself together. "Sorry," she said, her expression puzzled. She looked around the crowded room. "What'll it be? There's that table in the middle of the room or the booth way back in the corner."

Some choice, Annie thought, waiting to see which Nick would prefer. What he did was turn to her. "Annie? What's your pleasure?"

She could have strangled him. Slowly she turned her head to look at him. She *should* have strangled him, she decided when she saw the amusement behind his bland facade.

He and Connie waited. The whole room waited, or so it seemed to Annie. She cleared her throat. "Uhhh . . . why, I suppose . . . the booth?"

Connie's thin eyebrows arched toward the ceiling and she nodded. "A nice, quiet, out-of-the-way booth coming right up," she said brightly. "Follow me." She moved away, hips swinging.

Annie hesitated, casting about for some way out of this predicament. Nick leaned down to whisper in her ear. "Now, be brave. You're not running out on me."

The unexpected warmth of his breath sent little prickles coursing down her spine and she tightened her muscles to ward off a shiver. "I'm not running anywhere," she grated. "I'm not afraid of you, Nicholas Kimball!"

That was a lie, of course, but there was no way he could know that. Or so she consoled herself, until she heard his muffled laugh. She glanced up quickly, her cheeks burning, but he wasn't even looking at her. Instead, his assessing glance measured the room.

They reached the booth and she sat down, disgruntled. It was difficult to keep her expression smooth and unrevealing, but she tried. She couldn't let him think he was getting to her.

Which he was. She couldn't imagine what he wanted to talk to her about, but she was sure he was up to no good. She had to regain control of this situation, and would . . . just as soon as she caught her breath.

In the meantime, she looked around, recognizing the intense interest of practically everyone in sight. Darn Nick Kimball for putting her in this position!

Connie opened a menu, slapped it down in front of Annie and stood there, radiating curiosity. "Can I get either of you a cup of coffee?" she asked almost as an afterthought.

Nick gave Annie a questioning glance.

She shook her head. "I'll have a glass of iced tea, please." She closed the menu and slid it across the tabletop to Nick. If he thought she was going to break bread with him, he had another think coming.

He took the menu and handed it to Connie without opening it. "I'll have the same, followed by two steak sandwiches and two orders of those curly fries. Put a dip of chili and some cheese on one of 'em."

"Ugh," Connie said cheerfully, as if this were a game the two of them played often. "You got it, Nick." With a conspiratorial wink, she bustled away.

Annie let out the breath she hadn't realized she'd been holding. "That's a lot of food," she said. "I certainly hope you're hungry."

"I've been hungry all my life."

His mask of civility slipped, revealing a fierce determination that jarred her. Here was a man accustomed to having his own way.

She tried to keep her voice indifferent. "Good, because if you ordered any of that food for me, I'm afraid I'll have to disappoint you. When I say no, that's exactly what I mean."

He leaned back against the green vinyl bench seat, his gaze steady and thoughtful. "Even if your no was ill-advised?" He picked up a fork and turned it over and over in his hands without looking down.

She stared at him, mesmerized by the slow, easy motion. His fingers were tapered and flat-knuckled, the nails square and neatly trimmed. His hands looked powerful, and powerfully competent.

She jerked her shattered attention back to the conversation. "My father always told me, 'When in doubt, say no.'"

"Sounds like something a father would say." His glance caught and held hers. "Safe but boring."

She swallowed hard and looked away...finally. "Not at all." She cleared her throat. "That advice helps me avoid situations like this one." She sat up straighter and tried for a no-nonsense tone. "I had every reason to doubt the wisdom of joining you for coffee or for lunch or for...for anything at all. But you insisted. Now I'd like to know why."

His eyes narrowed. "You don't listen very well, do you?"

Annie bridled beneath his criticism. "I beg to differ. I'm a very good listener."

"Listening well and being a good listener are two entirely different things. I, for example, listen very well indeed—am, in fact, a professional. But no one has ever called me a good listener."

What on earth was he talking about? She felt as if he were addressing her in a foreign language. "Mr. Kimball—Nick, I don't have the first idea what you're getting at," she admitted with as much dignity as she could muster. "If you're trying to make me feel stupid, you're succeeding admirably. If you're trying to tell me something, you're failing."

"I'll be damned," he said. "You've finally managed to surprise me. I never expected such—"

"Two iced teas. Here you go, folks." Connie smacked the tall glasses down on the table. "Food's coming right up."

"Take your time." Nick seemed irritated by the interruption and didn't even glance at the waitress. He kept his attention on Annie, and she, embarrassed, dropped her gaze.

"Well, ex*c-u-u-use* me!" Connie flounced away.

Annie removed the wedge of lemon on the edge of her glass and placed it on a paper napkin. With clumsy fingers, she opened a small white packet of sugar and stirred it into her tea. Just as she inserted the straw and drew her first taste, he spoke.

"Hey, I'm sorry," he said.

She choked. His apology was so unexpected she swallowed wrong and a fit of coughing overtook her. When it passed, she looked up at him through damp eyelashes to see if he meant it.

He apparently did. His strong face with its cleft chin and high cheekbones looked completely sincere. "I never meant to make you feel stupid," he said. "Let me start over. Back there outside the store, when I first accosted you, I offered you a cup of coffee—"

"Which I tried to turn down," Annie inserted, just so he wouldn't think she was touched by his apology.

"True. But I also offered you a glamorous career in journalism. As far as I know, you haven't turned *that* down."

Annie felt as if he'd punched her in the stomach. Had he heard her practically begging Larry Rayburn for a job? Had Nick understood what she was really saying where Larry hadn't?

"What makes you think I'm interested in a job?" she demanded sharply.

He held up one hand in a placating gesture. "Take it easy. Why do you think I'm stressing the glamour?"

"I have no idea why you do anything you do."

Connie interrupted again, plunking down two heavy platters. "Chow's on," she announced. She slid one platter in front of Nick and the other toward Annie. "Anything else? Ketchup? Piece of pie? A chance to scotch the rumors flying around this room?" She gave an ain't-I-funny? laugh that fell flat.

Annie had been so engrossed with Nick that she'd momentarily forgotten the curious stares. Reminded, she shot him an agonized glance. Without thinking, she picked up a spiral of french-fried potato and nibbled unhappily.

Nick gave Connie a glance as icy as the frozen north. "No comment," he said, his voice a malevolent purr. "And the next time we're interrupted—"

"Nick!" Annie gasped. "For heaven's sake, don't—"

Connie hurriedly took a step back. "Right, privacy—you got it, Nick. You want me, give a call."

"Hold your breath," he invited.

Annie watched the waitress scurry away. A man seated in a nearby booth reached out to halt her retreat. He said something; Connie glanced over her shoulder, then leaned down and whispered behind a cupped hand.

Annie turned to Nick. "Now you've done it," she accused. "Everybody in this room's either watching us or speculating on what's going on."

"You think I'm enjoying this?" He picked up his sandwich and turned it this way and that, as if trying to decide where to sink his even white teeth. "Besides, you're exaggerating. There's a kid over there in a high chair who couldn't care less. Why don't you quit worrying about public opinion and listen to what I'm trying to tell you?"

"Because—" She picked up a knife and cut the sandwich in front of her in half. "Because this whole thing makes me so nervous I could scream. Everybody looking at me, you talking in circles..." She took a bite. At least eating gave her something to do.

"You want it in a nutshell?" He leaned forward, his expression aggressive. "How's this—we need a new society columnist at the *Bandwagon* and somehow Roz got it in her head that she wants you."

"Wants me for what?" Annie reached for another fry.

"The job." He frowned at her as if she were half-witted. "I'm offering you the job. With your contacts, it'll be a piece of cake. When do you want to start?"

All the confusion that had gone before was nothing to what she felt at that moment. Disbelief and indignation warred for supremacy as she stared at him, a curly french fry halfway to her mouth. What was he up to now? What could possibly be behind such a crazy proposition?

"You must be joking!" she finally managed to croak. "After what your newspaper did to my husband, you have the nerve—"

"Hold it right there." His eyes shot blue sparks. "The *Bandwagon* prints the news without fear or favoritism."

"And a piranha is a small helpless South American fish," she retorted.

"Pollyanna has claws. Good." He looked surprised and pleased. "Can we get past the name-calling? I'd like to talk a little business, here."

She subsided into stunned silence and he went on.

"This is the deal—you'll be responsible for the Sunday life-styles page. You've seen it, right? So you know what I'm talking about."

Annie picked up the second half of her sandwich. This couldn't be happening. "Certainly not. You know Robert cancelled your... newspaper."

Nick's lip curled. "Go ahead, call it a rag. I can take it."

She gave him her sweetest smile. "Rag, then. A rose by any other name... Whatever you call it, I don't subscribe."

He gave her a sour glance. "Okay, I'll spell it out, then. I'm talking about a social column, a full page weekly. But it's not as scary as it sounds."

It didn't sound scary to Annie, since she had no intention of getting involved with it. When he paused, she shrugged and pulled the platter closer. Hers was nearly empty. His was barely touched.

He curled his fingers around the iced tea glass as if it were a weapon. "You'll have to take your own pictures but we'll furnish a camera and instructions. Nothing to it—a trained chimp could pull it off."

"How flattering."

"Don't get touchy. You'll just go to all the places you go anyway, all the la-di-da social claptrap in town, and write up grammatically correct but otherwise purple passages about the people and the events."

She pushed away her empty platter. "You realize, of course, that I know absolutely nothing about journalism."

He waved that aside. "This isn't journalism, this is puff."

"Puff?"

He seemed surprised by her ignorance. "You know, puff, the antithesis of journalism. Words full of hot air."

"Oh, that's really nice. I'm not surprised you can't keep a social columnist with that attitude."

"Correction—social columnists, at least of the wanna-be variety, are a dime a dozen. I just can't find one who knows a participle from a predicate."

"You still haven't." Annie folded her paper napkin and laid it on the tabletop.

"Roz says you can do it. I've decided to give you a chance." He stuck out a hand as if to seal the deal.

Annie shrank back, snatching her own hands out of reach. "Give me a chance!" She nearly sputtered in indignation. "You cannot, in your wildest dreams, seriously believe I'd consider working for the *Bandwagon*. No one in *town* could seriously believe I'd consider working for the *Bandwagon*."

"Will you quit worrying about public opinion?" He shook his head irritably. "I'll admit, when Roz first brought up your name, I had a couple of reservations. Frankly, I doubted you'd be woman enough to do the job. But now I think I've changed my mind."

"You *think* you've changed your mind?" She gave him a haughty stare.

"Okay, okay, I've changed my mind," he said with little conviction.

"Well, I haven't and I won't, Mr. Kimball."

"That's a very selfish attitude, Mrs. Page."

Taken aback by his nerve, she glared at him. "How do you figure that? Just because I want nothing to do with your old newspaper doesn't make me selfish."

"Almost." He leaned back, a cynical smile on his well-shaped lips. "If you honestly cared about your community, you'd do this. You know all the right people—hell, you're *one* of the right people."

"Don't make it sound like a character flaw!"

He raised his brows. "Did I do that? Sorry. In my zeal, I may have gone overboard. But the fact remains, people enjoy seeing their names and faces in the newspaper. Here's your chance to make your fellow Buena Vistans happy."

She'd never thought of it that way. "You mean I'd get to—uh, the social columnist gets a free hand?"

"Certainly. Within the boundaries of good judgment, of course." He gave her one of those looks that said, "Don't you know *anything*?" "We want to hire your know-how, your judgment, brains and maturity."

Was he speaking tongue in cheek? His motives couldn't be pure, and yet . . .

"Look, it's just part-time. It won't interfere with your life-style," he went on without missing a beat. "You're already aboard the social and civic merry-go-round. It'll just take a few extra minutes to write it down." He gave her a crocodile smile. "You're perfect for the job."

She met his eyes, trying to discern the motivation behind his glib words. She wasn't tempted by his offer, not really, she assured herself. She clasped her trembling hands together and tried to remain calm. This was probably just one last attempt by Nicholas Kimball to discredit an old enemy by compromising his widow, she decided.

Furthermore, Nick hadn't mentioned money. Perhaps he thought she'd do it for the prestige. Prestige? *Ha!*

"I'm flattered...I guess," she said at last. "But it's out of the question. You understand."

His eyes narrowed to slits and his face hardened. A shiver of apprehension streaked down her back. This was the Nick Kimball she expected, the hard-edged arrogant man who threw around the power of the press as if he'd invented it.

"Hell no, I don't understand. Why is it out of the question? Because your husband didn't like me?"

Annie caught her breath, appalled by his bad manners. "I . . . why, I don't know what . . . that is . . ."

He looked as if his worst suspicions had just been proved true. "Relax, Annie," he said, his tone insolent. "I didn't mean to be quite that blunt, but the truth is, I didn't like him any more than he liked me. However, I did respect his right to be wrong. I can only assume from your reaction that he didn't extend that same privilege to me."

He was confusing her again, trying to put Robert in a bad light. She was glad she'd have the last word by turning down his wretched job. In fact, if he didn't stop harassing her, she might just forget she was a lady and tell him what she thought of his job, his newspaper . . . and *him*. "Leave Robert out of this," she commanded.

Nick gave a curt nod. "As you say. But before you give me your final answer about the job—"

"You've got my final answer," she exclaimed, wondering if he needed a brick wall to fall on him or what.

"—let's talk money. I'm not offering much, I'll admit. This is the Buena Vista *Bandwagon*, not the *Los Angeles Times*."

Oh, Lord, this is a paying job! She swallowed hard, suddenly weak with longing—longing to be employed. Guard down, she glanced across the room and a movement caught her attention. Three people sat in a booth, waving and grinning.

She could just imagine what they were saying: *"What on earth is Annie Page doing, sitting there with her husband's worst enemy?"*

Shaken, she turned back to her companion. "There's really no need to go on," she choked out, more anxious than ever to escape this public display.

"Let me finish!" He glared at her. "We're paying this current perpetrator a hundred-and-fifty dollars a week. I was ready to pay you two."

Two hundred? In real American dollars? Not a fortune, but it could make all the difference in her squeaky-tight budget. *No, don't weaken! You will not work for this man, now or ever,* she reminded herself. It was disloyal even to sit here with him.

His mouth curved up in a cross between a sneer and a chilly smile. "I see by your expression that you're not impressed. Therefore, I'm prepared to pay you ... oh, what the hell? Two-hundred-fifty a week, and that's tops."

One thousand dollars a month! She could have the plumbing fixed. She could have the car tuned. She could send Lew money for a new bicycle to replace the one run over by the car that also ran over him. She could pay her annual pledge to the Kids' Club. Oh, if only there were a way!

If only there were a way ... but as far as she could see, there wasn't.

CHAPTER THREE

BEFORE ANNIE COULD RESPOND, a murmur arose from the other customers. Looking around, she saw Rosalind Charles hurrying between the tables. Connie trotted behind the editor of the *Bandwagon*.

The waitress got in the first word. "I tried to stop her, Nick. Don't blame me." She held up her hands as if to ward off his displeasure.

Nick slid over so Roz could sit down.

"Hi," she said, giving Annie a big smile before turning toward her boss. "I'll bet I got a half-dozen calls in the newsroom from astonished Buena Vistans, wanting to know what the heck's going on with you two." She sounded pleased.

Nick looked annoyed. "Why not put it on page one?"

"I might. Depends on whether she said yes or no." Roz looked at Annie eagerly. "Well?" she prodded. "What's the verdict?"

Roz seemed so friendly and hopeful that Annie felt even more uncomfortable. "It was nice of you to recommend me, Roz," she said, "but I'm really not qualified."

Nick grunted disparagingly. "That's not why you turned me down. I think I insulted you by mentioning money. Crass of me. Really crass."

Roz expelled a heavy breath. "Nuts," she said. "Annie, please reconsider. Maybe Nick didn't make it sound as good as it is." She gave him a disapproving glare. "For one thing, you won't have to work with him, you'll work with me and Debbie. Now that's a plus."

"Debbie?"

"Debbie Darling. You may not know her. She's the society editor—the life-styles editor, as it's known nowadays. Nice girl. A little drifty, but you'll have no problem handling her."

Annie shook her head. "There's just no way," she said, wishing there were. She needed the money so badly her stomach clenched with wanting. But more surprising, she was becoming intrigued by the job itself. It *did* sound glamorous, as Nick had promised.

Curiously enough, she could understand their reasons for offering her the job. She did go to many of the social events in Buena Vista, and she did know an awful lot of people. She had written occasional news releases for the various organizations to which she belonged; she was self-taught, but the papers usually printed her little stories the way she sent them in. She must be doing something right.

And obviously, Roz had gone to bat for her. Annie had always liked Roz and now felt gratitude as well.

"Please?" Roz wheedled.

Annie sighed. She couldn't accept. She just couldn't. Robert would never understand. *The town* wouldn't understand.

"Just think about it," Roz urged.

"Well..." Annie struggled to find a nice way to say no. What a crazy situation, she thought, refusing a job she needed so desperately when she might never find another.

Nick lounged back in the corner of the booth, his eyes narrow and watchful. His lack of participation somehow annoyed her, but she tried not to let that show.

Just to be nice to Roz, Annie tried to soften her eventual but certain refusal. "Okay, I'll think about it," she conceded. "I suppose that's the least I can do, but it won't change anything in the end."

"Hallelujah!" Roz glanced triumphantly at Nick. "Gives me time to work on her, anyway."

Nick's lip curled. "Work fast," he commanded in a tone completely lacking in patience. "If we do this, I want it to be soon. I'd like to introduce Annie as our new social columnist at the Chamber of Commerce awards banquet a week from Saturday."

"Nick!" Roz looked horrified.

A feeling of inevitability settled over Annie. He'd made this much easier for her, she realized. She should be grateful. "In that case," she said, sliding to the edge of her seat, "the answer is no. I'm not even going to the Chamber banquet this year."

Mostly because she couldn't afford the ticket, but that wasn't any of his concern.

"The *Bandwagon* is sponsoring a table," Nick said in an offhand manner, as if he hadn't heard the word *no*. "You'll come as our guest."

Annie stood up. "No, thank you," she said, steel underlying her soft tone. She looked down at him. The man was a chameleon, but she knew the real Nicholas Kimball. Beneath the good looks and the occasional surface charm, he was the same man who'd waged a relentless war against her husband. She wouldn't be fooled again.

Roz held out a hand beseechingly. "Annie—"

Annie shook her head. She knew with absolute certainty that she had done the right thing, the only thing. "I'm sorry. Goodbye, Roz."

She turned away, took one step and halted. Good manners imposed certain standards. Bracing herself, she turned back to Nick. "Thanks for the lunch I didn't want," she said.

His lips twitched in an almost-smile beneath his mustache. His own food remained virtually untouched. "It was nothing. Trust me—you'll enjoy the dinner you don't want equally as much."

Annie felt as if everyone in the restaurant watched her walk away. The whole town would know of the incident by tomorrow, and it galled her to think about her name being bandied about.

She was behind the wheel of her car and headed for home before she could think rationally about what had just happened.

Winning the state lottery couldn't have surprised her more than a job offer from the publisher of the *Bandwagon*. If she wasn't such a sensible woman, she'd think she'd been hallucinating, for her husband and Nick Kimball had been adversaries almost from the beginning.

When the Pages moved to Buena Vista five years before, Robert was a lieutenant colonel in the Marine Corps with orders to Camp Pendleton. Within months, he was injured in a training accident that left him with a permanent limp and a medical discharge at the age of forty-four.

Annie, sixteen years his junior, cared for him with the same loving diligence she'd lavished on her mother. As he regained strength and confidence, he'd looked around for an outlet for his considerable energies.

Being Robert, he decided to start at the top; he'd run for mayor. He planned his assault on city hall like a military campaign—and he planned to run the city like a military operation once he won, which he was confident from the very beginning he would.

A handsome and imposing figure at the political forums despite his limp, he spoke with absolute authority on every subject. Annie, who never involved herself in politics, just smiled and stayed in the background, offering support and worrying about his health.

She'd been doing much the same thing all her life, first as an Army brat and then as a Marine wife. Where before she'd volunteered her time to Navy Relief and the Red Cross, now she turned to Lew's school, to the Kids' Club and the Cultural Foundation. One involvement led to another, and soon Buena Vista became the hometown she'd never had.

In the meantime, Robert approached Nick Kimball, the new owner and publisher of the *Bandwagon*, with wary caution. But life in the Marine Corps hadn't prepared Robert for the subtle realities of civilian politics, and soon he reverted to his usual manner of dealing with underlings—a manner long on orders and short on persuasion. It irritated Robert no end to discover his rank brought him no privileges whatsoever with the media, and discover it he did.

Quickly.

He found the reporters especially trying, "smart-mouthed kids" being one of his kinder tags for them. Their questions became more and more probing and therefore more and more objectionable. When it finally dawned on him that he couldn't control what they wrote about him, his anger and frustration flared out of control.

Annie didn't know exactly what happened the day he took his complaints directly to Nick Kimball. She only knew the result. When the *Bandwagon* endorsements came out, Robert was not among the chosen.

She'd always thought that was what made him angry enough to hit the streets in a last-minute effort to win votes. To the surprise of almost everyone, his strategy worked.

Election night, Nick walked up to the new mayor and held out his hand. "Congratulations," he said dryly. He looked like a man trying to make the best of a bad situation. "You didn't get my vote, but what the hell? Ten thousand Buena Vistans can't be wrong—I hope. How about a victory statement, your honor?"

Annie's heart sank. She knew Robert would bristle at the publisher's cavalier attitude.

Robert looked down at the other man's extended hand and gave a sharp, unfriendly bark of laughter. "I've got nothing to say to you, Kimball, now or ever." His lip curled. "As of this moment, the mayor's office is closed to the *Bandwagon*."

Nick's eyes narrowed and his expression turned wintry. He dropped his hand to his side as if sorry he'd offered it. "Don't try it, Page," he said with gentle malevolence. "There's an old saying in the media—never argue with the man holding the microphone. He'll always get the last word."

Annie stifled a groan. Robert would take the publisher's words as a challenge. She recognized the look on her husband's face, the vaulting self-confidence that he could take on a newspaper in hand-to-hand combat and win.

She touched his arm and smiled, a subtle plea to tread with care. He patted her hand but didn't look at her or alter the course he'd set.

"We've got old sayings in the Corps, too," he told Nick. "How about this one—nobody argues with the Pfc. except another Pfc. That's why I'm not arguing with you, Kimball. I'm *telling* you. Stay out of my way and I'll stay out of yours."

How naïve we were, Annie thought as she turned the car, its engine coughing and wheezing, into the curving driveway before her house. The day after the election, the editorial in the *Bandwagon* lambasted the closed military mind of the new mayor, dubbing him the "political Page."

Hostilities between the two men never ceased after that, occasionally escalating into sharp clashes. Robert denounced Kimball and his newspaper from the mayor's office; Kimball denounced the mayor and his policies from the pages of the *Bandwagon*.

And then, four years later, Robert died.

NOT KNOWING HOW to go about finding a reliable real estate agent, Annie called the city manager for guidance. Robert had been instrumental in selecting Mitch Priddy for the top city job, and the two men had become friends and political allies.

Mitch seemed happy to hear from her, but surprised by her request. "Real estate agent, huh? Funny you should ask. I've just been talking to one of those guys myself," he said.

"Moving up, Mitch?"

"Maybe moving on, if everything works out. I've been talking to Jack Bell at A-Number-One Realty. If you like I could ask him to contact you."

It had been that easy. Why couldn't finding a job be equally simple? It was so unfair that the one job she was offered, she couldn't accept.

Two days later, no closer to solving her problem, she headed home from a Cultural Foundation meeting. She'd put out a few careful job feelers around town but nothing had developed. She doubted anything would. Everyone seemed to share Larry's misconception that she merely needed a diversion.

I've just got to stop being so timid, she scolded herself. *It's time to get serious about finding a job.* She squared her shoulders and lifted her chin—just as her Chevrolet sputtered, coughed and died. Annie's stomach plummeted as she guided the coasting vehicle to a stop at the curb. If the car broke down, it could be the final nail in her financial coffin.

She turned the key in the ignition; nothing happened. She tried several more times with the same results. Fighting panic, she slumped back and tried to get a grip on her anxiety.

When she had, she opened the car door and climbed out. She didn't bother to lock the door behind her; with any luck, someone would steal the pile of junk and she could get the insurance on it.

If she had insurance on it, other than collision. Probably it was too much to hope that a train would run over it.

Feeling grim, she examined her surroundings. Nearby she could see a fast food restaurant, a small shopping center and a lumberyard. Home was a least three miles away.

She glanced down unhappily at her black, high-heeled pumps. She wouldn't get far in those shoes before she'd be hobbling. Should she simply call a garage? She knew absolutely nothing about cars, beyond how to pump gasoline into one. She'd have to believe anything they told her, and what if they took advantage of her lack of automotive expertise? To whom could she turn for advice?

A silver Toyota passed, slowed and pulled in at the curb ahead of her. Roz Charles crawled out with a cheerful wave.

"Hi, Annie. Got car trouble?"

Relief flooded through Annie. "I'm afraid so. I wonder... could you give me a ride home, Roz? These shoes weren't made for walking."

Roz glanced at the narrow-heeled pumps and agreed. "Glad to, if you don't mind going by my office first. I've got to touch bases with one of my reporters right away. I just got a hot tip from a usually reliable source."

"That's fine," Annie agreed gratefully.

"You haven't changed your mind, by any chance?" the editor asked hopefully as they buckled their seat belts. "The job at the paper's still open."

Annie wanted to burst into tears. She'd never felt so frustrated in her life. Desperate for a job, she still couldn't think of a way to accept the one that had fallen into her lap. Not and save face, anyway. "You just don't understand, Roz," she said miserably.

Roz pulled out into traffic. "I may understand better than you do, and I *sure* understand better than Robert did. Now that you're a captive audience, so to speak, I think I'd better explain the facts of public life to you."

Annie frowned. "I beg your pardon?"

Roz signaled a right turn. "Robert didn't know how to play the game of politics, Annie, and he wasn't interested in learning. He *did* enjoy a good fight with a worthy opponent, but he took the whole thing way too seriously."

She paused as if expecting dissent but Annie, unsure where this was leading, said nothing.

"Annie, the quarrel between Nick and Robert was pretty much a fifty-fifty proposition. The difference was, Nick's a professional. He knows how to disagree without being disagreeable, if he gets the chance. To the day he died, Robert didn't seem to understand that."

Annie's face felt stiff as parchment. "You're saying it was all Robert's fault?" she asked in a strangled voice.

"Not at all. I'm saying they were poles apart politically, so when Robert threw down the gauntlet Nick was more than delighted to pick it up. Made good copy, livened up the editorial page. Robert won an occasional battle but there was no way he could win the war. He couldn't even get a draw, not without eating a whole flock of crow.''

"He never learned to swallow his pride," Annie admitted, trying not to sound defensive. Roz only wanted to help. "I tried so many times to get him to—" She broke off, shocked by her own disloyalty.

"Me, too. With Nick, I mean." Roz pulled into the parking lot behind the *Bandwagon* offices. "My point is, why should you sustain this nonsensical quarrel?"

She guided the car into a parking space and killed the engine, turning to look Annie squarely in the face. "My teenage daughter calls remarks like the one I'm about to make sexist, but I'll say it anyway. Annie, it's up to us women to show men how to climb out of the holes they dig for themselves."

Annie laughed in spite of the seriousness of the subject. "What are you suggesting, Roz?"

"That you give my esteemed publisher a second chance. Let bygones be bygones and come to work as the social columnist for the *Bandwagon*."

Annie's smile slipped. "Oh, I don't think that's a good idea."

Roz reached out to touch Annie's hand lightly. "But it is a good idea," she said. "Annie...I know."

Annie felt blood rush into her cheeks, even though there were a million things Roz might "know." "Wh-what are you talking about?" she forced herself to ask.

"I'm talking about your financial problems. It's nothing to be ashamed of, for heaven's sake. What do you think *I'm* working for—love? Sure, I've got a great job, but I also need that paycheck, just like everybody else. I've got one kid in college and another headed in that direction if she can just drag up those grades a notch."

"But how do you know? About me, I mean." If Roz knew, who else might know? The bitter taste of humiliation filled Annie's mouth.

"I'm a journalist, remember? It's my business to know these things." Roz gave Annie's hand a last, comforting pat. "It's also my business to keep secrets. So you don't need to worry. I haven't said a word to Nick or anybody else, and I won't. I just don't want you to let stubborn pride and misplaced loyalty force you to pass up this opportunity."

"I couldn't work for Nick Kimball." There, she'd placed the responsibility squarely where it belonged.

"Don't be ridiculous," Roz shot back. "Nick's a terrific boss and a fine newspaperman." She opened her car door. "I've always liked you, Annie Page. If you can get past your prejudices, I'd enjoy working with you."

She got out and leaned down to look inside the car. "I'll just be a minute. Think it over while I'm gone. When I get back I'm going to ask you one more time, and if you say no, I won't belabor the issue further. But I will be disappointed."

Roz walked away and Annie settled back to wait, her emotions in a tangle. Everything Roz said made perfect sense. But work for Nick Kimball...could she do it? Dared she do it? Would Robert understand?

The side door of the *Bandwagon* building opened, and Nick and two other men appeared. They paused just outside the door, deep in conversation.

Annie slumped in her seat, praying he wouldn't notice her. She didn't want to face him after the way she'd walked out on him at Hoffy's. Maybe she'd hurt his feelings and he'd never speak to her again even if their paths crossed. Maybe—

The two men hurried back inside the building and Nick turned toward the parking lot. His glance zeroed in on Annie, and she groaned out loud. With purposeful strides, he approached her open car window and leaned down.

"Roz says you've got car trouble," he announced. He wore a blue-and-green polo shirt that clung lovingly to his well-muscled chest and swelling biceps. "I said I'd take a look."

"I wouldn't want to bother you," Annie said primly. She tried to pry her glance away from the fascinating cleft in his chin and succeeded in raising her glance to the level of his mouth. When he smiled, she swallowed and looked away.

"Roz said you'd say that, but I can handle a reasonable amount of bother," he announced, opening the car door and grabbing her arm. "I'm pretty good with cars and I don't mind showing off." He pulled her to her feet and hustled her along in front of him. "You know the old joke..."

"What old joke?" She resisted but he propelled her effortlessly past parked cars. She felt powerless to resist him and it wasn't a feeling she enjoyed.

"The carburetor won't carb, the generator won't gen, and the pistons don't...work. Lucky for you, my specialty is pistons."

He halted beside a sleek black pickup truck. Inserting a key in the lock, he threw open the door.

She edged away. "There's no need for you to go to all this bother," she asserted somewhat breathlessly. She didn't like the way he was taking charge, as if it were his right to do so. "I'll just call the Auto Club."

"If you belonged to the Auto Club, that's the first thing you'd have done." He advanced on her. "What are you so nervous about? Relax."

He reached for her, his hands like lightening. Soothed by his voice, she had no time to react. She felt his fingers press into her waist and tighten as he lifted her off her feet. With a little cry made up of equal parts shock and alarm, she grabbed for his shoulders.

He held her high, laughing up into her face. Stunned, she stared into guileless eyes as clear and blue as lake water. She was afraid to struggle—not afraid he'd drop her but afraid he wouldn't.

"You're a hard woman to figure out, Annie Page," he murmured. "I don't understand what makes you tick...or why I should care."

"You shouldn't," she gasped. She felt as dizzy as if she were dangling from a ten-story building. "Put me down, Nick. You have no right..."

For a moment he simply smiled at her, his expression at once questioning and beguiling. Then he swung around and deposited her inside the cab of the truck. "Be sure and buckle up," he instructed as he closed the door.

Annie did his bidding, her hands trembling so badly she could barely fit the two halves of the buckle together.

NICK CLOSED THE HOOD of Annie's Chevrolet and gave it a satisfied pat. "All set," he announced.

Annie, watching from the sidewalk, stared at him. "You mean that's all? You fixed it?"

"You don't have to sound so surprised."

He rubbed his hands together but the oily streaks didn't disappear. He'd also picked up an ugly black stain across the front of his nice knit polo shirt, Annie realized.

"You've ruined your shirt," she said. "I'm sorry."

"I said I was a good mechanic. I didn't say I was neat." He cocked his head to one side, a quizzical expression on his face. "Don't you want to know what was wrong?"

"Not really," she admitted, "unless it's something that's likely to happen again."

"It isn't. If it does, call me."

She couldn't imagine doing that, ever. "Thank you. I...I'm really very grateful." Feeling ill at ease, she looked down at the ground. It was a strange feeling, being beholden to Nick Kimball.

"Are you?"

"Of course." Her surprised gaze flew to his face. "If there's ever any way I can return the favor..."

For a moment he stood there with one hand on the hood, his expression speculative.

If he asks me to take the job now, what'll I say? Annie wondered. Her heart began to bang a painful rhythm against her ribs.

But all he said was "Thanks. I'll remember that." He turned toward his pickup.

"Nick."

He stopped short. Slowly he turned. "Yes?"

Annie bit her lower lip. What should she do? she wondered uncertainly. Should she mention the job herself? "Do you...do you really think I could do the job for the *Bandwagon*?"

She held her breath, waiting for his answer. He seemed to consider very carefully before he spoke.

At last he said, "Roz thinks so. When she brought your name up, I thought she was—is crazy too strong? But in all the time we've worked together, I've never known her to be wrong in her assessment of people. On the strength of that, I finally let her talk me into offering you the job. I didn't figure it mattered—I was sure you'd turn it down, which, in fact, you have. Several times."

"I see." The disappointment she felt surprised her. She knew what Roz thought, but she'd wanted to know what *he* thought. Now she did. "At least you weren't disappointed." She managed a weak smile. "Thank you for your honesty. And thank you for fixing the car. I'll be happy to replace the shirt you ruined helping me."

"I don't care about the shirt." He took a quick step closer and looked into her eyes, his own suddenly blazing. "This time I'm not talking for Roz, I'm talking for me. Annie Page, can I interest you in a glamorous job in journalism? I can offer you long hours, low pay and no fringe benefits except a hell of a lot of fun. What do you say? Last chance—take it or leave it."

Annie stared at him, her heart in her mouth. Could she...dared she...might there be some way to accept and keep her self-respect? If only she understood his true motives—and then she realized his motives weren't the issue, hers were. And her motives were simply to use Nick's money to protect Robert's memory.

There couldn't possibly be anything disloyal in that. "I'll take it," she said breathlessly. And because she didn't know what else to do to cover her relief and excitement, she extended her right hand, hoping he wouldn't notice how it trembled.

For a moment he stared down at it. Then, almost reluctantly, his own big hand enveloped her small one. A prickle of excitement shot up her arm, but she forced herself to ignore it, lifting her eyes to meet his gaze.

He shook his head slowly. "If I hadn't heard it myself, I wouldn't believe it," he said in a tone of wonder. "Who says the age of miracles is past?"

CHAPTER FOUR

EVERYTHING FELL INTO PLACE the minute Annie accepted the job at the *Bandwagon*.

Jack Bell was happy to list the house whenever she gave the word, which she'd do once she figured out a gentle way to tell Lew. In the meantime, Lew called to say his cast would come off earlier than expected, and he'd return to his part-time job in another week.

Best of all, Annie would soon begin receiving a paycheck. Oh, glorious day! Standing in the *Bandwagon* newsroom at the start of her orientation tour, she smiled in anticipation just as Nick walked past.

He frowned, gave her a perfunctory wave and kept walking. Disappointed at his lack of enthusiasm, she stared after him.

Roz looked up from her explanation of the wire photo machine. "What's the matter?" she asked.

"I don't know," Annie admitted. "Nick didn't look happy to see me."

"He's just busy. One thing you need to remember about Nick if you're going to work here, Annie. His bark truly is worse than his bite." Roz looked thoughtful. "Although his bite can be pretty bad, too."

That's supposed to comfort me? Annie wondered as she followed Roz into a room filled with light tables and mysterious machinery.

Roz gestured expansively. "This is where the pages are pasted up," she explained. "It all comes together here."

Dutifully Annie followed, through composing, through the camera room where photos were transformed into halftones and where negatives and plates were made, and into what Roz called "the back shop," where big offset presses rolled.

Annie concentrated hard. She had the feeling Nick still wasn't entirely sure he'd done the right thing in hiring her, so she had a lot to prove. Besides, the job added an excitement to her life she hadn't even known was missing.

After touring the circulation department, only the photo lab remained. As Annie and Roz approached the darkroom, Pete Petersen loped up, a bulky camera bag flopping against his side. Two cameras hung from straps around his neck.

Roz drew Annie forward. "You two know each other?"

"Sure." Pete accepted the hand Annie offered. "We go way back—I see her all over town."

"Then perhaps it won't surprise you to learn Annie's taking over the Sunday social column," Roz said. "You photo-guys'll be souping her film. You can give her the old Pentax and check her out on how to use it."

"Sure thing," he said with a friendly grin. "Welcome aboard, Annie."

He fished a key from his pocket while Annie read the sign on the door: "Darkroom—Don't open the door without knocking or all the dark will leak out."

He gestured her forward and Annie stepped inside, looking around curiously. She'd never been in a darkroom before and was surprised at how orderly it was. An L-shaped counter with several large pieces of equipment took up two walls. A clock was mounted prominently on a third wall, over two large, shallow sinks.

At the far end of the room, black strips of film of various lengths hung from a line, anchored by clips. Canisters dangled from the ends of the film like little anchors.

Pete started divesting himself of equipment, just as the phone on the counter rang. He grabbed the receiver and listened intently, then said, "I'm on my way."

He hung up and gave the women an apologetic glance. "Sorry." He grabbed the camera bag he'd just set on the counter. "Fire—sounds like a good one. Catch you later!"

He bolted out the door. Watching him, Annie felt her heart beat faster. It was exciting to be among the first to know. She hoped the fire wasn't a serious one, but she also hoped Pete's pictures would be wonderful. She could hardly wait to get tomorrow's paper and find out.

That realization brought a rueful smile to her lips. She was actually beginning to feel loyalty to the *Bandwagon*. Amazing. But no more amazing than the softening of her attitude toward Nick. To her own astonishment, she was developing a grudging respect for the strong-minded publisher.

Respect, nothing more. She still didn't feel at ease around him, perhaps because he seemed to have pegged her as some kind of society snob. But the way things were going—

Roz's sigh derailed that train of thought just in time.

"So much for camera classes," the editor said philosophically. "Photography is not my strong suit. I guess we'll have to reschedule."

Nick walked through the doorway. "I'll take over, Roz."

Roz shot him a startled glance. "I thought you had an important—"

His brows lowered. "Don't think, Roz."

He stood aside to let her pass. She gave Annie a wide-eyed shrug and departed.

Annie fiddled nervously with her skirt and waited. She couldn't imagine why Nick would use his valuable time to give beginning photo lessons, but hers was not to reason why.

He walked inside the small room with a smile she interpreted as cautious. As always, he seemed to dominate any space in which he found himself. She edged away.

"I take it this is your last stop on the tour," he said. "Any questions so far?"

She shook her head, little more than a reflex action.

"Then let's plunge right in." All business, he opened a metal cabinet. "This is the camera you'll be using. It's a 35 mm SLR with—"

He handled the camera with the ease of long familiarity. He'd rolled up the sleeves of his white shirt, exposing sinewy forearms—she yanked her attention back where it belonged. "I'm sorry," she blurted. "What's an SLR?"

He frowned. "Single-lens reflex. Maybe first I'd better find out how much you know about photography."

She laughed sheepishly and spread her arms in a helpless gesture.

"That much." He grimaced. "Okay, I'll keep it short and sweet. You'll get your film from us—we use black and white Tri-X. Our photographers will load the camera with either ten or twenty-four exposures. You tell us which you want, depending on where you're going. We buy film in hundred-foot rolls and load the cassettes ourselves."

He paused, looking at her as if expecting questions.

Mesmerized by the sound of his voice she took a minute to respond. When she realized he was waiting for some reaction from her, she nodded hastily, wondering what on earth she'd been thinking about. Certainly not about cameras.

"You'll have to learn to set the shutter speed and f-stops," he added matter-of-factly.

"You can't be serious!" She gave him a look of pure disbelief.

"I'm quite serious. I'll make up a chart for you—bright sunshine, shoot 1/400 at 16. That's 1/400 second shutter speed, f-stop 16. With a flash indoors, shoot 1/60 at 11—nothing to it. You'll learn it by rote." He frowned again. "Of course, back lighting throws everything off, but we'll worry about that later."

Annie's throat tightened. Somewhere along the line she'd missed something, the part supporting his contention that this was going to be easy. "It's all beginning to sound highly confusing," she said anxiously. "Are you sure I'll be able to handle it?"

"Absolutely. Piece of cake." He spoke with certainty. "You won't even have to think twice about it after a week or two. What you *must* think about, from day one, is focus. Only aging Hollywood actresses benefit from soft focus, which is just another way of saying out of focus."

He glanced at her for assurance that she was still with him, and she nodded quickly. Nick Kimball wasn't turning out to be at all like she'd expected, and in the relative closeness of the darkroom, those discrepancies were making her exceedingly tense.

He held out the camera with one hand, pointing to the last ring on the protruding lens with the other. "This is the focusing ring," he said.

She gave him a blank look; she hadn't been paying attention to what he was saying, only to the way he said it. She'd never known anyone as confident as he appeared to be, not even— "I don't think I can do this," she said. "I'm getting confused."

"I can see that." He cocked his head to one side and drew an impatient breath. "Here," he said suddenly. "I'll show you."

Before she knew what he was doing, he caught her arm and swung her around in front of him. He stepped up close, too close, his arms slipping around her. He leaned forward and his chest pressed lightly against her shoulder blades.

She opened her mouth to protest, just as he lifted the camera up in front of her face. His forearms brushed the tips of her breasts in passing, sending a crazy jolt of excitement knifing through her.

"Look through the viewfinder," he instructed. "There—can you see anything?"

Too shocked to answer, she stood in the circle of his arms, stiff as a post. He surrounded her, psychologically as well as physically. *This is insane,* she thought. *I have to get out of here.*

He nudged her with his shoulder. "Hey, you in there, wake up. Can you see anything through the viewfinder?"

"Oh!" Flustered, she tried desperately to follow his instructions while ignoring her feelings—which she couldn't have put a name to anyway. "Y-yes, but—"

Holding the camera before her, he caught her right hand in his and guided it up until her fingers fumbled against the focusing ring. She felt like a lump of ice, all cold and clumsy and brittle.

"That's it," he encouraged, his mouth very near her ear. "Turn that ring until everything's in focus."

It was torture but she forced herself to do his bidding. Slowly the image drew together until she could see something that looked like a giant camera, mounted in a frame and pointing down.

She licked dry lips. "Okay," she whispered. "It's in focus, but what is it?"

"An enlarger. I'll show you how it works."

He stepped away from her and placed the camera on the counter. Annie all but collapsed with relief. She wasn't used to being handled so casually—after all, it had been a year since Robert's death. Well, maybe "handled" was too strong. But touched. She certainly wasn't used to being touched, not by anyone.

And—her breath caught—she'd missed it. She stood in the middle of the room, numb all over, while Nick closed the door. What, if anything, had just happened? Was she out of her mind or did the very air sizzle with tension?

The room plunged into darkness.

"Oh!" She couldn't stop herself from crying out in alarm. But even as her nerves betrayed her, a red light pierced the total blackness.

"Safe light," he said. He moved with perfect assurance, the light turning his white shirt crimson. "Now watch. I place the film in this holder—" he fitted actions to words "—and I put the holder in the enlarger. Now I flip the switch."

He glanced back at her, his expression that of a teacher dealing with a not-very-bright student. She swallowed hard and nodded. The unearthly red glow added to her sense of unreality.

"Come over here so you can see," he ordered, grasping her hand to draw her forward. "The light goes through the film, through the lens, and ends up down here, as an image on the white easel. I can focus the film two ways, by..."

Mind whirling, she looked down at her hand in his, scarcely even glancing at the ghostly image coming into focus on the flat white surface below the lens of the enlarger.

He probably didn't even realize he still held her hand in his. He probably took similar liberties with every woman he met and thought nothing about it. He was, after all, a man of the world.

While she... she was little more than a country bumpkin, by comparison. Sure that anything she might do would be misconstrued, she forced herself to do absolutely nothing.

"Annie? Annie, do you understand?"

At his sharp question, she jerked her head up to look at him. He leaned toward her in the ruby glow, dark brows raised in inquiry.

She didn't understand anything, not anything at all. Least of all did she understand why she was reacting to the man and not the boss. So she lied. "Yes, of course I understand."

"Good." In the eerie light, his face took on a devilish cast. "Because I could have sworn you were a million miles away."

Which she devoutly wished were the case. She needed to get out of here, away from the enforced intimacy of the darkroom with its bizarre red atmosphere.

But most of all, she needed to get away from Nick. Abruptly she stepped back, her heel coming down on something that rolled beneath her foot. She stumbled and felt herself falling—right into his arms. He whisked her upright and held her against his chest, so tightly she could feel the thud of his pulse beneath her cheek where it came to rest at the base of his throat.

She couldn't seem to catch her breath, a reaction she dimly realized was somewhat out of line with the minimal amount of danger she'd been in. Clinging to him, she castigated herself for such weakness.

"You okay?" His husky voice raised goose bumps on her arms. "People who aren't used to darkrooms have to be careful."

She gave a shaky laugh. "Careful is my middle name. I don't know what's the matter with me. I . . . I'm not usually so clumsy."

"I hope not. I wouldn't want to lose you."

"L-lose me?" With a lifetime of self-discipline to draw on, still she found herself on the verge of panic.

"Lose you before you even write your first column," he elaborated. He touched her chin lightly with his fingertips and tilted her face up.

In the strange lighting, his eyes were fathomless dark pools. Dangerous dark pools. "Nick," she whispered unsteadily, "don't—"

"Nick, don't you think you better let me in? I've got to soup this film!"

The pounding she heard wasn't her heart at all; it was Pete's fist on the darkroom door.

Nick settled her onto her feet and released her. "Hold your horses, Pete!" he called.

He switched off the safe light and switched on the regular light, then threw open the door. Pete stood there, one fist still raised.

"Oh, hi," he said. "Sorry to interrupt—" he glanced curiously at Annie, standing rigidly erect in the middle of the room "—but this is hot stuff." He waved a camera. "Big fire in a trash bin behind city hall. Got a shot of the city clerk trying to put it out with a garden hose."

Annie felt as disoriented as if she'd just awakened from a dream. Remorse flooded through her at such an idea. *Make that a nightmare,* she corrected herself.

Nick scowled at the photographer. "Hold the presses," he said sardonically.

"Hey, it gets better." Pete began unloading equipment. "She turned the hose on our esteemed city manager—strictly an accident, she claims, but Mitch got just as wet as if she did it on purpose."

Nick's nod was surly. "Then we'll get out of your way and let you go after that Pulitzer Prize. Annie?"

He looked at her with raised brows and she took a hasty step toward the door. He picked up the Pentax and followed. She wanted to run from the room; she forced herself to walk.

"Let me see contact prints," she heard Nick call back. To her, he added, "We'll finish up in my office. Don't want you to leave with any questions."

Questions? Good grief!

She had plenty of questions, all revolving around a few crazy minutes in the darkroom when she'd let her imagination run away with her. Nothing had happened; all she had to do to confirm that was look at Nick. He walked along beside her with perfect nonchalance as they made their way through the corridors.

Once in his office, he sat behind his desk and Annie took the chair beside it. It was going to be all right, she told herself as he explained camera settings. He even wrote instructions in a reporter's notebook: 1/400 at 16, 1/200 at 16, 1/60 at 11. *Yes,* she thought. *I can do that.*

He handed her the narrow notebook. "Run a few rolls of film through the camera and see what you get," he advised. "You'll soon catch on to the correlation between these settings and the end result."

"Isn't that a waste of film?" she asked, ever the thrifty one.

He shook his head. "Annie, Annie, Annie. Film is cheap, compared to losing an opportunity. Think about it—you're at a party and take two shots of the guest of honor."

She nodded. "So? What's wrong with that?"

"What if one shot is out of focus?"

"Then we use the other one." Why was it suddenly so natural to refer to herself and the *Bandwagon* crew as "we"?

"And what if our guest of honor has his eyes crossed in the other one?"

Annie grimaced. "I guess I have to call him up and ask if I can try again?"

"Very good. Of course, it won't be in the context of the party—that's gone forever."

"I see what you mean," Annie admitted. "But something's better than nothing."

Nick's grin broadened. "True. But in this case, even that won't work. Our guest of honor's secretary tells you he just left with his beautiful wife, Rhonda, on a six-month, around-the-world cruise. So what do you say to that?"

She sighed. "Film is cheap?"

He nodded. Just then Pete strode through the open office door, waving a sheet of contact prints over his head. Nick gestured to Annie to join him while he leaned over the miniature photographs, peering through a magnifying loupe.

Mitch Priddy's dignity was going to suffer, but even Annie had to admit Pete had captured some funny shots. Nick offered her the loupe and she picked up the sheet. The city manager's outrage and the city clerk's remorse brought a reluctant smile to her lips. She also noticed that Pete had taken nearly two dozen shots.

Nick drew a heavy circle with a red felt-tipped pen around one shot. "Page one."

"You got it, boss." The photographer bustled out.

Annie frowned. "Is that necessary? It'll be embarrassing enough for Mitch without being on the front page."

Nick leaned back in his big leather chair, his brows lowering. "This is probably the first time a stringer ever questioned my news judgment," he said flatly.

"What's a stringer?"

"You are. One who strings along, a part-timer." He sounded annoyed.

"Oh." She felt properly chastised but went on doggedly. "I don't mean to question . . . what did you call it, your news judgment? But Mitch really is a nice man. I hate to see him held up to public ridicule."

"We don't make the news, we only print it." He cocked his head to one side and fixed her with an unsmiling gaze. "Why so protective?"

Annie felt her cheeks flush. "I'm not," she denied. "It's just that he was a friend of Robert's and I like him. Besides, he did me a favor a few days ago and I'd like to return it if I can."

"By talking me out of putting him on page one?" Nick's brows rose. "You can't, so forget it. Tell him you tried, if you want to make points." He looked at her with curiosity. "What did our esteemed city manager do for the mayor's widow?"

"He recommended a real estate person, that's all."

"You selling your house?"

"Isn't that usually why you need a real estate person?"

"And Mitch recommended . . . ?"

"Jack Bell." She gave him a deliberately saccharine smile. "I'm surprised at your interest. Don't tell me *you're* planning to move, too?"

He laughed and changed the subject. By the time she left five minutes later, she'd all but forgotten the exchange.

NICK STARED out the window for a full five minutes after Annie had gone, his expression closed and thoughtful. Then he picked up the telephone and dialed Roz's extension.

"I think our city manager is about to jump ship for a new job," he told her. "Have Curtis check for a listing on his house with Jack Bell at A-Number-One Realty. If that pans out, confront Mitch himself... You know better than that, Roz. Just put it down to a couple of usually reliable sources."

ANNIE CLASSIFIED the enjoyment she got out of reading the *Bandwagon* under the heading of guilty pleasures. Every time she went out to her driveway to bring in the paper, she felt a remorseful thrill, as if she were doing something delightfully wicked.

In fact, her loyalties were being severely tested. Although she tried her best to hold herself aloof from the general camaraderie of the *Bandwagon* staff and specifically from the charismatic publisher, she found that harder and harder.

The day after her tour of the newspaper building, she found her loyalties even more severely tested when the picture of Mitch Priddy turned up on page one. She had to admit it was funny—the middle-aged city clerk with an expression of horror on her face as the stream of water bounced off the chest of the flabbergasted city manager.

So okay, Annie argued with herself, the picture wouldn't dampen anything except his dignity. Robert would have been outraged, of course, but maybe... just maybe Robert had been wrong in taking such an aggressive attitude toward the press.

And if he was wrong about that, might he not also have been wrong about Nick, at least partially?

Two days later, she found something much more difficult to rationalize. *Buena Vista City Manager Finalist for University Job,* the banner headline screamed across the top of page one. And a mug shot—she remembered the newspaper terminology—of Mitch Priddy.

With trembling hands, she carried the paper inside and spread it on the small kitchen table.

"...city manager refused to confirm or deny...is known that the university is seeking...spokesman would only say that Priddy is a finalist for the job...announcement expected Friday...according to a local real estate agent, Priddy's house will go on the market Friday...."

Annie balled the offending page into a crumpled mess. Her last conversation with Nick exploded in her mind. But surely he wouldn't...he couldn't....

She dialed Jack Bell.

"Gosh, Annie, I didn't know what hit me," he complained. "A guy called and said he was interested in buying the big gray house in the middle of the 700 block of Adobe Road. How was I to know it was that clown Curtis from the *Bandwagon*? I would have lied if I'd had time to think but...he outsmarted me, I guess. Although how they tracked me down I'll never know."

Annie knew, to her shame.

She dialed city hall.

"I'm sorry, Annie, but Mr. Priddy is out of the office," his secretary said. "Shall I ask him to call you?"

"I'd appreciate that, Judy." Annie hung up, figuring she'd better not hold her breath waiting. Probably he didn't want to talk with anyone right now.

She fully expected Mitch to react to the story the same way Robert would have—with total fury. The relationship between local government and the press was adversarial at best. Every time the paper dug up and printed a story officials wanted suppressed, it made matters worse.

For a moment she considered keeping her mouth shut concerning her own culpability; no one would ever know.

No one except Nick Kimball. No one except Annie Page. Sitting there at her kitchen table, she wrestled with her conscience.

She'd really begun to look forward to her job, and not just because of the paycheck. Her confidence had grown by leaps and bounds. She'd been practicing with the camera, reading the paper front to back every day, and . . . her head drooped . . . slowly changing her opinion of the publisher.

Prematurely, it now appeared. He'd left her no options. She was morally bound to quit.

I must have let my good judgment be swayed because I found him . . . somewhat attractive, she thought. *Okay, so I'm human. But that doesn't mean I'm going to associate myself with a man lacking in principles and a rag that perpetrates yellow journalism!*

Yellow journalism—Robert had been right after all.

WHEN ANNIE ASKED to speak to Nick, the receptionist at the *Bandwagon* looked surprised. "Why, sure," she invited. "Employees can go in any time the door is open."

Annie figured she'd qualify as an employee for approximately two more minutes. She thanked the young woman and marched to the doorway. As she paused there, Nick glanced up and saw her.

He looked so attractive with his dark hair falling over his forehead, and a big smile on his face, that she had to remind herself why she was there. She straightened her shoulders and lifted her chin a fraction higher, in defiance of the way her pulse accelerated. She wouldn't be deterred, even though she wanted to cringe at the prospect of a confrontation. She simply had no choice.

He stood up, his relaxed pose giving way to narrow-eyed caution. "What is it, Annie?" He glanced at the camera in her hands. "Bring in some film?"

"I brought in my resignation."

She crossed the room, shoved the camera into his chest and let go. He caught it before it could fall.

"What the hell!" He laid the camera none too gently on his desk and glared at her with a mixture of outrage and bewilderment.

She stood her ground, determined to face him bravely. "You took something I said in confidence," she accused. "You used it as the basis of a newspaper story and I'll never forgive you."

"Rash words." An icy wariness seemed to settle over him. "As the rattlesnake said, you knew what I was when you picked me up."

"What's that supposed to mean?" Her voice rose, shaming her. She mustn't lose control.

He sat back down, his eyes cold and watchful. "A woman put a rattlesnake in her pocket and he promptly bit her. 'Why did you do that?' she asked. 'Because I'm a rattlesnake,' he replied. 'You knew what I was when you picked me up.'"

Annie groaned. "Not even *I* was prepared to call you a rattlesnake, but the simile is certainly apt."

He gave her a grin without any warmth. "I'm a newspaperman, which in some circles is even lower. You knew what I was when you threw in with the *Bandwagon*. I print the news without fear or favoritism. I've told you that, so why are you surprised?"

"Because you betrayed my confidence," she said, her jaws so tight she had difficulty forcing out the words.

"That wasn't a confidence. I'd never betray a confidence. That was an idle comment. It just happened to click with a rumor I'd been hearing around town—that the city council had given the city manager a choice, resign or be fired."

"But—" She frowned. "That wasn't in the story."

"No, because we couldn't confirm it. But we could confirm the rest of it, once we knew where to look. You gave us that key, but I didn't realize it until you'd gone and I started putting two and two together."

"That's not fair!" She put her hands on the back of a chair and leaned forward earnestly. "Mitch is a nice man. He doesn't deserve this."

Nick made an impatient slashing motion with one hand. "I can't overlook news simply because it involves nice people, or friends of yours. Or friends of mine, for that matter."

"Mitch Priddy is no friend of yours." She knew this wasn't the first time Nick's paper had printed stories revealing things Mitch wanted kept under wraps. She'd conveniently forgotten how cutthroat the media could be. Ashamed, she turned toward the door. "This is hopeless. You'll have to find a replacement for me because I can't—"

"The hell you can't!"

He sounded close to losing his temper. She stopped short, although she didn't turn around. "Because I'm a lady, I'll try to overlook your blatant attempts to browbeat me," she said in a quivering voice.

She heard a wrathful purr behind her. "Maybe you're right. Maybe you should quit. I need a *woman* for this job, not a lady."

It was the last straw. She whirled on him. "Oh, you make me so—!"

Triumph flared on his face and she sputtered to a halt. Her cheeks burned with embarrassment, but she refused to give ground. "It's possible for me to be both, you know," she said in a trembling voice. "At least, it was until I met you!"

"It's a contradiction in terms. A woman goes after what she wants, while a lady waits for it to come to her as her due. A woman's not afraid to show honest emotion, but a lady is more interested in keeping her dignity intact than in anything else."

"You're wrong! A lady is more interested in keeping *everybody*'s dignity intact. It's called good manners, and it's nothing to be ashamed of." She realized she was moving toward him aggressively and pulled herself up short. She took a deep breath. "Well, now you've done it. You've made me lose my temper and forget my manners. I hope you feel good about it because I feel awful. My dignity is in shreds and so is my association with this newspaper." She turned to go.

"Hold on a minute!"

Annie halted at his command. She felt giddy from the rush of adrenaline through her bloodstream. She couldn't remember the last time she'd acted so precipitately.

Nick's mouth turned up at one corner in a cynical line. "If you're not *woman* enough to honor your commitments, I won't try to talk you into staying. But I will teach your ladyship a few cold hard facts before you march out of here in high dudgeon."

As he spoke, he picked up his telephone and dialed. "You know," he said conversationally, holding the receiver to his ear, "Robert would be proud of you. You're acting just as bullheaded as he ever— Yeah, hi, Judy. Mitch there? It's important."

CHAPTER FIVE

ANNIE STARED at Nick in horror. How could he face Mitch, even over the telephone? "What on earth are you doing, returning to the scene of the crime?"

Nick covered the mouthpiece with one hand. "Prepare to eat your words," he advised. Hastily he withdrew his hand. "How's it going, Mitch?" A big grin. "Yeah, got you fair and square, didn't we." He glanced at Annie. "I've got someone here I want you to repeat that to. Mitch, say hello to our new society columnist."

Nick thrust the telephone toward Annie. Automatically she stepped forward and accepted it, her stomach churning. She couldn't imagine what was going on, and said a very tentative "Hello?" into the receiver.

A short silence, then, "Annie? Annie Page, is that you?"

"Y-yes." It really was Mitch; she couldn't believe it. "Mitch, I want you to know how sorry—"

"I'll be darned. Then the rumors are true—you're going to work for the *Bandwagon*. That's great."

She frowned, turning away from the man behind the desk. She didn't want to look at the canary-eating expression on his face. "Yes. I mean, I was, but now everything's changed. I...uh, I..."

"What are you trying to say, girl?"

"That it's all my fault," she blurted, trying to keep her voice low enough that Nick couldn't hear. She was willing to humble herself, but preferably not before him.

"What's all your fault?" Mitch sounded confused.

"That story. I can't tell you how sorry I am. I never dreamed he would take an innocent remark and—"

"Wait a minute, wait a minute. What're you talking about?"

"The story in today's paper. I was talking to Nick Kimball about something totally different the other day and stupidly mentioned you'd recommended Jack Bell to sell my house."

"And the wily devil put two and two together. Well, I'll be— I wondered how he figured it out."

Was that *laughter*? "Mitch, I won't work at a newspaper that practices yellow journalism," she avowed with dignity. "I just quit."

Silence. She began to wonder if the connection had been broken. "Mitch? Are you still there?"

He sighed. "Annie, keep the job. You'll be great."

"How can you say that, after what they did?"

"Because that's the way things are done in the real world. Where do you think newspapers get stories? Look, I don't want to be put in the position of defending a newspaper. Lord only knows I've had my differences with the lot of them."

"Then why are you so calm?"

"Because, Annie dear, I've been in the public eye long enough to realize that all's fair in love, war and the pursuit of a scoop. Nick earned this story, and I've got no beef with him. It happens to be true—I do have another job. It'll be announced Friday. Nick stole our thunder, but what the heck—he's got his job, I've got mine. Sometimes they're at odds, but there's no need to get personal about it. I'm just relieved he didn't find out about—"

He stopped speaking abruptly and chuckled. "Oops. Better leave well enough alone."

"Mitch! You don't think I'd spill the beans twice!"

"I don't even blame you for spilling the beans once. I just hope you reconsider about working for the *Bandwagon*. You'd be a good influence on all those hard-bitten news types. We need someone on the inside who's also on *our* side."

"Thanks for the vote of confidence, but I already turned in my camera." And maybe foolishly, she admitted to herself. Good grief, how could she have overreacted like that?

"Hey, Nick Kimball never takes no for an answer," Mitch assured her, "at least not the first ten or twenty times he hears it. Do us all a favor and let him talk you into staying."

"Yes, well, I'll think about it," she replied, purposely vague. "In the meantime, good luck with your new job."

She stood there in Nick's office, hearing the disconnected buzz of the telephone and wishing she could begin this day all over again. She had prejudged Nick. She hadn't given him a fair chance. She'd just remembered how Robert would have reacted and condemned the *Bandwagon* and its publisher without so much as a hearing.

Unfortunately, there wasn't a thing in the world she could do about that now. Even if she crawled, she couldn't expect Nick to give her a second chance. Why should he? She hadn't given him one.

She would apologize, though. That was the least she could do.

Nick cleared his throat. "Well? You plan to hang up that telephone or just stand there hugging it all day?"

She turned slowly to replace the receiver on its cradle. For a moment she stared at it and then forced herself to face him.

His mouth quirked up at one corner beneath the luxurious mustache. "I don't suppose you'd like to tell me what 'beans' Mitch didn't want spilled this time?"

At her outraged gasp, he shrugged. "I didn't think so. In that case, let's get right to it. What'll it be, Annie? Will the woman fulfil her commitment to this newspaper in a mature, responsible manner, or will the lady crumble the first time she doesn't get her own way?"

She bit her lip. "You make me sound like a spoiled brat. It's not fair to—" She broke off on a gasp. Could he be offering her another chance? "You want me to *stay*?"

"That's right. I want you to stay."

Could she? Did she dare, with everything becoming so complicated? *Go for it,* the woman in her whispered. *You'll be sorry,* the lady warned.

The woman won.

"Then I'll stay." Her voice sounded unexpectedly firm. "The lady in me apologizes for rushing in here like a crazy person—"

"Crazy may be a tad too strong." He looked pleased but quickly hid it. "Or then again, maybe not."

"Will you let me finish, please?"

He nodded with an air of mild repentance. "I stand corrected."

She needed to say it all, before she lost her nerve. "The woman in me warns you never to do that again." It came out half order and half plea.

"Do what?"

"Take some innocent comment and blow it all out of proportion."

His expression was puzzled, but then he laughed, and shook his head ruefully. "Annie, you've got a one track mind. Okay, I'll make you a promise—if you ever tip me to anything again, I'll tell you before I use it."

She felt a great surge of relief and said a heartfelt "Thank you."

He followed her to the door. "Don't misunderstand. I'll never ask your permission, I just won't surprise you. Okay?"

She paused in the doorway. "I guess it'll have to be okay."

He reached out as if to pat her shoulder, but at the last instant dropped his arm to his side. "Don't look so glum. It's a better deal than anyone else ever got out of me."

She gave him a look full of doubt and turned away.

"Don't forget the Chamber of Commerce banquet Saturday," he called after her.

She drove home, not sure whether she'd pulled off a coup, cut her own throat, negotiated a reasonable compromise or been outmaneuvered. And despite the undeniable fact that she needed the money, she had a sneaking suspicion she'd really stayed because of Nicholas Kimball.

She took some consolation in the possibility that she might just want to be around when he went too far.

HE WENT TOO FAR Saturday night—all the way to Annie's house. She'd just pulled on her Good Black Dress when the doorbell rang.

She tugged at the zipper as she hurried to the front door. She already had on her panty hose but not her shoes, and her feet slipped and skidded on the entry tile. Her thick dark hair curled over her shoulders, not yet pulled back in the severe style Robert had favored.

She grabbed open the door with one hand, smoothing down her skirt with the other. "I'm sorry—what can I do—?"

Her downcast glance settled on gleaming black patent leather shoes topped by what could only be tuxedo trousers . . . worn, she saw with horror as her gaze climbed, by Nick Kimball. He stood before her with an expectant expression on his face. He looked all freshly barbered and brushed and gleaming in his elegant black tuxedo, and she caught just a whiff of some woodsy and manly after-shave.

He gave her a wary grin, his teeth a flash of white beneath the dark mustache. "Ready to go?" he asked.

"Ready? Ready!" She took three steps backward and her hands flew to her unconfined hair. She curled one unshod foot around the other. "Do I appear *ready*?"

He seemed to take that as an invitation to decide for himself. His blue eyes assessed her, beginning at her stocking feet, sliding up her sleek legs like a caress, lingering over the swell of her hip and the curve of her waist— stopping cold at the thrust of her breasts.

She forgot to breathe. Beneath his bold appraisal, she felt her nipples tighten and knew they must be visible beneath the black silk. Just when she felt she couldn't stand another second of his perusal, his glance moved on, up her throat with its wildly beating pulse, to her lips, parted in consternation.

"Leave your hair down," he suggested softly.

"M-my hair?" She caught her breath, her hand smoothing her unruly mane. "You didn't even look at my hair!"

He stepped into the hall and closed the door behind him. "No?" He raised his brows innocently. "What was I looking at, then?"

Things that don't concern you, she thought. She answered his question with one of her own. "Nick, what are you doing here?"

"I've come to take you to the Chamber of Commerce party." No one could be as innocent as he pretended.

"Afraid I wasn't going to show?" she accused. "I said I would."

"And I believed you...sort of. You're a woman of your word. Mostly." He advanced and she retreated. "Do you plan to ask me to sit down or do I have to stand here in the hall twiddling my thumbs while you do...whatever?"

"Neither. Listen, I don't want to hold you up—"

"Too late," he interrupted.

She gave him a scathing look. "*As I was about to say,* you go ahead to the party and I'll come along when I get ready. I promise."

He shook his head, a familiar stubborn expression settling over his face. "I'll wait."

"Nick!" She clenched her hands into fists and glared at him. "I don't want to be rude but—"

"Go ahead." He shrugged shoulders that were impressively broad. "Won't do you any good."

He unbuttoned his tuxedo jacket and sauntered past her, into the living room. After a disgruntled moment, she followed. She didn't know why his presence in her home felt like a total betrayal, but it did.

He paused inside the door and looked around. "You sure as hell don't believe in dust catchers," he remarked.

"What?" She gazed over the room, seeing it through his eyes. It looked empty and cold. She'd long since sold the good pieces of furniture, and packed away all items with sentimental value as part of her desperate need to stop living in the past.

The result was a room that looked as lonely and un-
loved as its mistress felt. But it was rude of him to draw
attention to it.

"I...it's just that—wait a minute!" She stopped short,
frowning. "Don't change the subject. You have no right
to be here."

"Sure I do." He sat down on the beige couch and
crossed his long legs. He looked up at her expectantly.
"It's the Golden Rule—the man with the gold makes the
rules. You're a guest at my table at this party."

"But-but—"

"Don't sputter, Annie," he suggested, his voice mild.
"Your job came with strings attached and this is one of
them. I'm going to announce your professional association with the *Bandwagon* tonight. I want you there.
Otherwise, who'd believe it?"

He leaned back with exaggerated ease. "I get restless
when I'm kept waiting. Get moving, will you? We're
missing the champagne reception."

"Ohhh!" Annie turned and almost ran out of the room.

What a nerve that man's got! she fumed as she stomped
down the hall to the master bedroom. The thought of
spending the evening in his company was almost more than
she could bear. She shivered. And just when they'd been
getting along so well, professionally speaking.

She grabbed a brush and dragged it through her hair.
The large round tables at this event seated ten, so she
needn't worry about being the object of his attention all
evening. She felt sure that once he made his announce-
ment, he'd lose interest in her.

She gathered her hair into one hand, preparing to twist
it up at her nape...and hesitated, remembering the way
he'd looked at her minutes earlier. Her breasts still tingled, and she felt a tight little ache in the pit of her stom-

ach. She released her hair and fluffed it out. Her hands were shaking too badly to pin it up; she wasn't doing this to please him, not at all.

She took a deep breath and gave her image in the mirror one final critical glance. Her hair fell in soft waves around an unusually pale face. Her dark eyes glowed with a suspicious brightness beneath their swooping brows, and her mouth trembled.

But the thing that struck her hardest was the vulnerability she saw in the face of that woman staring back at her. That woman could be hurt too easily.

An optical illusion, she assured herself as she slipped her feet into simple black pumps. She couldn't be hurt if she remembered who she was and why she was there.

As she reached for the small black evening purse, she heard a step in the hall. She caught her breath and her heart stood still. She'd lived alone long enough that the sound of another human being in the house filled her first with fear and then with longing. Nick's voice, coming from the other side of the closed door, broke the spell.

"Annie, are you about ready? They're drinking our champagne, even as I speak."

"I'm coming." She grabbed the purse and hurried to the door. *What will this evening bring?* she wondered. *How will the good citizens of Buena Vista take my defection to the enemy camp?*

When she opened her bedroom door and found that enemy smiling down at her, she forgot all about the good citizens of Buena Vista.

EVERY YEAR the Buena Vista Chamber of Commerce held the annual awards banquet at the Buena Vista Country Club. Every year, the event began with a champagne reception.

Annie and Robert had always skipped that part of the evening to arrive just in time for dinner. Robert didn't like champagne; he didn't like wine at all and Annie got into the habit of refusing it as well.

Therefore, when Nick offered her a glass of the bubbly, she automatically shook her head.

"Don't be ridiculous." He thrust the glass toward her. "This is California wine. Unless you're declining for moral or medical reasons, it's your duty to support the economy."

She took the glass, careful to avoid contact with his fingers. "You sure throw that word *duty* around a lot," she retorted, taking a sip. She hadn't tasted champagne in years, and the golden liquid tingled pleasantly on her tongue.

"With you, that's about the only thing I've found that works."

The president of the Chamber of Commerce rushed up and Nick turned to greet him. Annie tried to fade back into the crowd but Nick would have none of it. He drew her forward, including her whether she wanted to be included or not.

And that was the way it went. Everyone seemed eager to have a few minutes with the publisher of the *Bandwagon*, and a constant stream flowed around Nick and Annie. She grew accustomed to the questioning glances and the outright curiosity, relaxing a little when she realized Nick would shield her from the necessity of explaining why they were together.

He wouldn't, however, let her revert to her normal mode of behavior in such circumstances—a polite smile and a gently murmured disclaimer. The first time it happened was with Mike Andrews from the Kids' Club.

Leave it to good old outspoken Mike to declare, "I really got a kick out of that picture in the paper of the city manager and the garden hose. Reminded me of a mongoose facing a snake." He laughed. "I've got to admire the way you newspaper people manage to be in the right place at the right time." He gave Annie a look that asked, don't you agree?

Caught by surprise, she managed a strained smile. "Yes, well, they do seem to have their ways," she agreed dryly.

Mike would have let it go at that, but not Nick.

"Tell him what you really thought of the picture, Annie," he challenged. The dimples at the corners of his mouth deepened.

Mike's brows shot up. "Do I detect a difference of opinion here?"

"No," Annie said, just as Nick said, "Yes."

"Well, which is it?" Mike asked. His laughing glance swung from one to the other. Then both men looked at Annie.

She sighed. "Okay, it's yes and no," she admitted. "No, I didn't admire how they managed to get that picture and spread it all over page one . . . at first."

"At first?" Nick rocked back on his heels, pretending great surprise.

"Oh, all right, I thought better of it," she conceded grudgingly. "It *was* a good picture."

"Followed shortly by a good story," he pushed. "C'mon, Annie, admit it. Once you get past the emotion—"

"Ahem." Mike cleared his throat. "I thought when I saw you two walk in here tonight that the war was over. Now it appears even the cease-fire is in danger."

He winked and walked away, still chuckling.

Annie looked at Nick and frowned. "Now see what you've done," she accused. He'd already seen her at her worst, so it seemed unnecessary to censor her honest reactions quite so much.

"Hey!" He spread his arms wide and lifted his brows. "Innocent as a newborn babe." He glanced around at the thinning crowd. "Let's see if we can find our table before they start serving. I'm starved."

She followed as he cleared a path for her through the crowd of elegantly dressed men and women. She'd never known anyone quite like Nick Kimball. His aggressiveness put her off, but she also found him unexpectedly intuitive.

She'd better be careful or she'd also find herself without any secrets, she thought as she slipped into the chair he held for her. She'd go to any lengths to keep from giving him more ammunition to use against Robert's memory. She smiled across the table at Roz, seated next to her husband. Curtis Harvey, the city reporter, sat to Annie's right, his date on his right.

Nick sat down and picked up his wine goblet. "Cheers," he said, looking around the table. He saluted Annie with his glass. "To the *Bandwagon* team, and especially to our newest member, Annie Page. Long may we prosper."

Even Annie could drink to that.

"ANNIE PAGE, they told me you were sitting at the *Bandwagon* table and I didn't believe them!"

At the sound of a scornful voice, Annie looked up into the hostile eyes of Josephine Turnquist, wife of Buena Vista City Councilman Harold Turnquist. Harold seemed to have taken up the feud with the newspaper where Robert had left off.

Josephine was simply the latest of a long line of people who'd found one excuse or another to walk past the *Bandwagon* table, near enough to make sure that really *was* Annie Page consorting with the enemy. Some stopped to chat a few minutes and others just galloped by, staring. All combined to make Annie so nervous she could barely taste her hotel round of beef.

None, however, had been as confrontational as the councilman's wife, who now glared down as if personally affronted.

Annie opened her mouth to respond, but what could she say? She *was* consorting with the enemy.

Nick leaned over her shoulder, placing one big warm hand on her arm in a comforting gesture. "How's it going, Josy?" He gestured to Curtis, who was taking everything in with obvious interest. "Get this all down, Curt."

"Huh?" Curtis frowned, then brightened. "Oh, yeah, sure, boss." He pulled a reporter's notebook and a pen from the inside pocket of his jacket and posed as if ready to write.

Nick gave Josephine a bland smile. "You were saying?"

She pulled back a step, her narrowed glance settling on Curtis. "What's he doing?" she demanded.

"What he's paid to do—writing down every dim-witted thing prominent local citizens say and do." Suddenly Nick wasn't smiling. "If it's fact, it goes on page one. Opinions go on the editorial page." His voice dropped to a dangerous purr. "And I'm the one who gets to decide which is which. Now, you were saying something to my date about—"

"Date!"

Annie and Josephine gasped the word simultaneously.

"Why, sure." Nick's fingers dug into Annie's arm and his bland expression never wavered. "Date—a person with whom one has a social engagement. Surely you're familiar with the concept."

"I . . . I . . . yes, of course. I-it's . . . I have to be going." Josephine backed away a few steps before turning to flee. Her solid bulk collided with a skinny waiter and she nearly flattened him against a pillar.

Nick gave Annie's arm a reassuring squeeze before releasing it. "I knew a life-styles editor who used to scream about the witches and the bitches. There goes a woman who's a double threat."

Curtis guffawed, the sound snapping Annie out of her shocked trance.

"*Date?* What is this date stuff?" she demanded. "This isn't a date, it's business. Dating's for kids."

"You mean, kids as opposed to women of mature years who've lost their appetite for beef?"

Her throat closed, she stared at him without comprehension. "I . . . what—?"

He spoke with exaggerated patience. "Beef." He pointed to her plate. "You're not going to eat that, right? Mind if I help myself?"

While she gaped at him, he lifted the slab of roast beef off her plate and onto his own.

He picked up his knife. "As always, I stand by the dictionary," he said gently. "Will you pass the horse-radish sauce, please?"

She passed the sauce, wondering what her reputation would be like by tomorrow. She seemed to feel waves of disapproval breaking over her head. After this, she wondered if anyone would want her to come to their social events, even with the prospect of newspaper publicity.

She stared down at her plate, wishing she hadn't come, wishing she'd never laid eyes on Nick Kimball. She knew public opinion shouldn't matter so much to her, but it did. It always had. It was the yardstick against which her father had measured everything, including his daughter.

"Cheer up, Annie."

She flinched at the compassion in Nick's low voice. "I'm cheerful," she said in a tone of doom.

He sighed and put down his knife and fork. She noticed he'd eaten only a few bites.

"I'm sorry if I embarrassed you," he said. "That woman gets on my nerves—always has. Believe me, she doesn't speak for the majority of the people here tonight."

"No?" Her skepticism slipped through. "It's been my experience that people... Oh, never mind." She picked up her fork and poked at the peas on her plate.

His hand closed over hers and her fork clattered onto the plate. Her eyes, wide and vulnerable, flew to his face. He wasn't smiling, but his expression was...almost tender, she realized with shock.

"What?" he asked gently. "What has your experience been?"

"That when the going gets rough, people tend to bail out on you." She stared at him, aghast that she'd revealed her inner feelings so readily. But now that she'd begun, she couldn't seem to stop. "Whenever I've taken a step beyond the prescribed boundaries, I've always found myself out on that limb alone."

He was silent for a moment. Then he said, "You've been hanging around with the wrong crowd. But if the opinions of a few snobs are that important to you—then okay." He turned back to the food on his plate.

His voice was pitched low enough that she was sure no one else heard. She tried to match his level tone.

"Okay what?" She looked at him. In profile, his strong face seemed almost melancholy.

"Okay, I'll redeem you with your public." A new note appeared in his voice, adding a certain flippancy. "I'll make it clear to one and all that you are not my date, Mr. Webster be damned."

She glanced around to see if anyone was listening but their table mates seemed intent on other matters. "I appreciate the thought but how do you plan to do that? Go table to table?" She bit her lip, realizing how snippy she sounded. "I'm sorry," she added, misery consuming her. "You're the only person I know who consistently makes me forget my manners."

He turned his head, his eyelids half-lowered over knowing blue eyes. He gave her a lazy smile. "I'll take that as a compliment."

His eyes really were beautifully shaped and outlined with dark, thick lashes. It was a moment before she could pull herself away from contemplation of them. "Wh-what?"

He arched one brow. "I suppose I could go table to table, as you suggest, but I've got a better idea."

Thoroughly alert again, not to mention thoroughly alarmed, she straightened in her chair. The thought that hit her was so horrible it sent her mind reeling. "Not in the newspaper!" she exclaimed. "You wouldn't—?"

He laughed and his eyes sparkled dangerously. "That's a thought, but not what I have in mind."

Behind him, a man bustled out on the stage and began to adjust the microphone. Nick stood up, wadded his napkin into a ball and tossed it on the table.

"I'll do it right now," he said, sounding very pleased with himself. "Don't go away."

Annie jumped to her feet. Several people glanced at her curiously. Embarrassed, she sank back down and watched Nick stride away.

Turning toward Curtis, she beseeched him: "He wouldn't, would he?"

Curtis grinned. "I have no idea what you're talking about, but I can say one thing without fear of contradiction."

"What's that?"

"There's not much he wouldn't."

"Oh, my Lord."

With sinking heart, Annie watched Nick mount the steps to the stage. He leaned down and said a few words to the man at the microphone, covering the sensitive instrument with his hand. Then he moved around to adjust the mike stand.

He observed the crowd with a look of satisfaction on his face. Annie, sensing impending disaster, rose to her feet and tried to drift unobtrusively toward the exit. She could avoid seeing him, but she couldn't avoid hearing him.

"Good evening, ladies and gentlemen. My name is Nick Kimball and before we get into tonight's program, I want to make a few things perfectly clear."

A twitter of interest rippled through the audience. Annie walked faster, keeping her head down and hoping no one would notice her. Unfortunately, several waiters bearing heavy trays of dirty dishes blocked her immediate exit. She looked around, frantic to escape, and her glance met Nick's across the crowded room.

"Annie Page is not my date," he announced. "She *is* the new social columnist for the *Bandwagon*."

A collective gasp erupted. All eyes turned to follow Nick's glance and settle on Annie, who at that precise moment wished she'd never been born.

Nick spoke into the unnatural hush.

"And one more thing you may not know about Annie...she's Buena Vista's Citizen of the Year. Come on up and get your plaque, Annie, and let your grateful community say thanks."

CHAPTER SIX

ANNIE STOOD FOR A MOMENT in stunned disbelief as great waves of applause broke around her. *They really do like me,* she realized with a kind of wonder as people rose in a standing ovation. A magical path opened across the enormous room, leading straight to Nick. Smiling, he stepped away from the microphone and held out his hand.

She'd had it drilled into her from childhood that a lady never showed her emotions in public. But by the time she reached Nick, tears were streaming down Annie's cheeks. It seemed the most natural thing in the world to put her hand in his and let him lead her up the steps.

He guided her to the microphone and drew a sheet of paper from his pocket. Annie, eyes blurred with tears, could barely see the audience as he began to speak.

"What can you say about a woman—no, a *lady*—who works so tirelessly for her community? Annie Page is on the board of directors for five philanthropic organizations, serves on three city committees, does volunteer work for..."

Annie brushed at her damp eyes and drew a trembling breath. Never in her wildest dreams had she expected such a tribute.

And delivered by Nicholas Kimball, of all people. Her heart swelled with gratitude as she glanced his way. He chose that very moment to smile at her. Dazzled, she returned his smile without restraint.

He looked back at the audience. "Ladies and gentlemen," he said, "I give you Buena Vista's Citizen of the Year—the *Bandwagon*'s newest columnist and a woman known and admired by all of us in this room."

He drew Annie toward the microphone. "I give you Annie Page."

The room erupted with sound. She stood there, reveling in the outpouring of love that flowed over and around her, feeling warm and safe. When Nick would have stepped back to let her enjoy the spotlight alone, she clung to his hand and kept him beside her.

Only much later did she realize with a guilty twinge that she hadn't thought of Robert a single time during the ceremony.

"GOOD NIGHT, NICK. Good night, Annie. Congratulations again!"

Annie waved a weary hand toward the last of her well-wishers, the hand not holding the two-foot-tall Citizen of the Year trophy. Nick touched her elbow lightly, guiding her into his BMW. With a sigh, she collapsed against the soft leather upholstery.

He slid behind the wheel and turned his head to look at her. In the dim parking lot lighting, she could see the ghost of a smile on his lips. The upper half of his face remained in shadow.

"Surprised?" he asked.

She nodded. "But you weren't."

He started the car. "No."

"I guess that proves you can keep a secret," she teased. "Not everything shows up first in the newspaper."

"You'd be surprised, the secrets I keep." He guided the car out into the street. "Annie, can I ask you a serious question?"

"Sure." She rolled her head to the side so she could look at him. She'd toasted her award with several glasses of champagne, and now felt light-headed and just a little dizzy and tingly.

"Why do you do it? All those boards, all those clubs, all those volunteer hours . . . what's your motivation?"

She sighed. "You seem to forget, Nick. I have nothing but time. With Lew away at school I need—" the warm haze around her cooled and lifted just a bit "—something to keep me occupied."

He nodded. "Okay, but you didn't begin any of these activities in the past year. Why'd you do it *before*?"

"B-before?" Valiantly she tried to hang on to her happy glow.

He turned the BMW onto her street. "When you came to this town, you had a husband and teenage son. I can understand why you'd be so involved now. What I don't understand is—"

"Please don't say any more." She sat upright and scooted around in her seat. She had no intention of explaining to him that both her father and her husband had been ambitious men who saw nothing wrong with using the woman in their lives to get ahead. They'd seen her volunteer work as something to enhance their own prestige.

Nick guided the car into her driveway, braked and switched off the engine. "Everybody deserves a private life and I don't see when you've had time for one. Didn't it drive your husband crazy, not having you to himself?"

"No, of course not." She gripped her trophy so tightly her hands ached.

"It would me," he said, his voice low and intimate. "You're a very beautiful, sexy woman, Annie. Especially when you let your hair down."

She didn't want to hear this, didn't want to feel that sensual tightening in the pit of her stomach. She knew what it was, heaven help her—a sensual awareness that made her scalp tingle and her breathing labor.

It was a purely sexual response, and as such, seemed a terrible betrayal. Frightened, she took refuge in indignation. "For your information, Robert was very proud of my contribution to the community," she flared.

She wanted out of there. Fumbling for the door handle, she dropped the trophy and it rolled off her lap to the floorboards. "Now look what you've made me do!" she cried.

He bent down, retrieved her award and handed it to her. "You know what they say about all work and no play. You don't want that to happen to you."

His fingertips skimmed the curve of her jaw. She held her breath, unable to resist when he bent toward her. At the first tentative brush of his lips on hers, she froze. Both fight and flight were beyond her capabilities; shocked to the depths of her being, she submitted, sitting there with her eyes open wide in numb disbelief.

What was he thinking of? What was he doing? His soft lips and bristly mustache offered an intriguing combination unlike anything she'd ever encountered. He seemed in no hurry; with agonizing slowness, he cupped her face between his hands and tilted her head to one side.

"Even *I* need a private life," he murmured, as if that thought had just occurred to him.

His mouth sought hers in earnest. Never in her life had she been kissed with such thoroughness. She felt drunk, not with wine but with amazement. *How long has this been going on?* she wondered, praying for the strength to resist him. The sharp metallic angles of her trophy pressed into her, an uncomfortable reminder of all that stood between them.

He lifted his head and she heard his ragged breathing. In the shadowed confines of the car he stared into her face, frowning, his hands still framing her cheeks.

"Annie," he began, her name a question.

Reality hit her a nearly lethal blow. "Don't say anything! Please, don't." Chagrined, she threw open the car door and scrambled out. Weakly she leaned back against the cold metal, raising one hand to scrub across her tingling lips.

She hadn't expected to be interested in another man for years and years—maybe never. Certainly she'd never expected to be beguiled by her husband's worst enemy. After tonight, with the imprint of Nick's kiss still on her mouth, she could no longer deny the attraction that flashed between them. At least, not to herself; she'd deny it to him to her last breath.

She heard his car door open and flung herself forward toward her house and safety. He was around the vehicle in a trice, grasping her arm.

"Hold on!" He barked out the command. "What did I do, kiss the lady instead of the woman?"

"You have no right to kiss either one." She refused to look at him. She couldn't take a chance she'd weaken.

His fingers dug into her arm. "You want to explain that? Because if I ever saw a woman ripe for kissing..."

She groaned. "Don't say any more. Let me go—I'm humiliated enough already."

"*You're* humiliated?" His laugh sounded bitter. "One lousy kiss—what did I do wrong?"

"It wasn't lousy at all. That's the problem!" She whirled to face him. "I'm not capable of having a cheap affair," she cried, her cheeks aflame. "If that's what you have in mind—"

His outraged roar shocked her into silence. "Cheap affair?"

She couldn't tell if he objected to the suggestion of an affair or the word *cheap*. She shook her head miserably. "I'm not in your league and I know it. What else could you possibly want from me?"

His face, illuminated by the glow of the porch light, had become that of a stranger. "I wonder myself," he snarled.

Before she knew what was happening, he turned her around and hustled her up the porch steps. She fumbled her key from the bottom of her purse and he took it without a word, inserted it in the lock and pushed the door open. Returning the key to her cold hand, he looked down at her.

"Your first column will run two weeks from tomorrow," he said with frigid indifference. "Today, I guess, since it's past midnight. If you have any questions, talk to Roz."

"A-all right."

"Congratulations on your award. I hope it keeps you warm at night." He took her cold hand in his. She tensed, but he lifted it easily to his mouth. Again she felt that unwelcome thrill at the soft-harsh combination of his lips and mustache. He released her abruptly and turned away without a backward glance.

She stood there clutching her trophy until his BMW rounded a curve and passed out of sight. Then she walked inside and closed the door. What an awful end to a fairy-tale evening. She closed her eyes to counter the hot flood of tears she would not shed.

A hollow *thunk* brought her back to the present and she looked down, surprised to see she'd dropped her trophy.

ANNIE'S FIRST COLUMN in the *Bandwagon* was . . . well, all right, she supposed. She'd attended three events: a tea at the Women's Club, a ninetieth-birthday party for a Buena Vista pioneer and a fund-raiser for the Buena Vista High School band.

Although her heart hadn't been in it, she'd dutifully taken the names of attendees, snapped photographs and soaked up all the color. She sat up at the breakfast bar in her kitchen almost all of one night writing the column—directly on the typewriter, not first in longhand and then typed; she'd seen the way the professionals worked. Although it was difficult, she was determined not to take that extra step with pad and pencil.

Her prose wasn't what she'd have liked, but Debbie Darling, the life-styles editor, seemed surprised and gratified by the results.

"Hey, this is great," Debbie declared enthusiastically after reading the first two paragraphs.

"Read it all before you commit yourself," Annie suggested nervously.

Debbie laughed. "I can tell in one paragraph, Annie. You double-checked spellings of all the names, right?"

"Yes."

"That's great. Come by Friday afternoon and we'll do cutlines."

Cutlines? It took Annie a second or two to realize cutlines were the captions beneath the photos.

She was feeling pretty good about the whole thing until she saw the pictures. The page was already pasted up—columns of type on a full-sized dummy sheet, the halftone photos in place.

Several of the pictures were slightly out of focus, she realized with horror, and the exposures she'd used at the Women's Club must have been wrong because everything was so dark you could hardly tell one woman from another.

Annie groaned and turned stricken eyes on Debbie. "This is awful. I'm so sorry!"

"It ain't good but it's not the end of the world," Debbie said bluntly. "You'll get better. Good grief, Annie, this is your first page. What do you expect, perfection?" Shaking her head, Debbie retreated back into her office.

Annie stood at the light table staring down at the first edition of the Society Page, mortified. Maybe she couldn't do this after all. It was entirely possible that Nick and Roz had misplaced their confidence.

Suddenly her scalp prickled and she stiffened, knowing instinctively that Nick had walked up behind her. She'd seen him several times since the Chamber of Commerce party and had been shocked by his casual attitude. He had changed her life with that kiss; she'd never again be able to deceive herself into believing that she wasn't flesh and blood just like everybody else.

He, on the other hand, seemed constant as the North Star—and just as far out of reach.

"So what do you think?" he asked.

"I think if I were you, I'd fire me," she said, meaning it. "These pictures are awful. Out of focus, bad exposure and just plain dumb—everybody standing there shoulder to shoulder and saying 'cheese' into the camera."

Nick stepped up beside her. She tensed, the ease that had been developing between them a distant memory. She resisted looking at him, although she couldn't control her searing awareness of his lean, hard body.

"Look," he commanded, pointing to a picture of a teenage boy toting at least a half-dozen band instruments. "That's a terrific shot."

Annie leaned forward, frowning. "I hadn't noticed that one," she admitted. It really wasn't bad—sharply focused, good exposure. "Must be an accident," she decided. "Look at the rest of this mess."

Nick gave a disgusted grunt. "You have a nasty habit of concentrating on the bad and completely overlooking the good," he said impatiently. "It's not your most endearing quality."

"I'm not trying to endear myself to you," she said haughtily. She looked at him through lowered lashes. "I'm just embarrassed. I expected to do better."

"We all learn from our mistakes—if we're smart, anyway. Quit flirting with me and get your notebook. We'll go over this page line by line, photo by photo."

"Flirting! Why, I never—"

The expression on his face had changed. Too late, she realized he was teasing her.

Or was he? Annie found it nerve-racking to stand next to him, only the smallest part of her uneasiness caused by his minute examination of her mistakes. He had a wonderful way of making everything on the page seem impersonal and she might have relaxed, had she not been so excruciatingly aware of him—the timbre of his voice, the dimple that flashed in his cheek, the occasional brush of his shoulder against her arm.

He might criticize the work but he never criticized the worker. By the time they finished, she had a vast new respect for his journalistic expertise. Grudgingly she admitted to herself that it was this very professionalism that had earned him the respect and affection of his employees. But how to reconcile this side of Nick with the side Robert had known? The two men were fire and ice—

Roz stuck her head through the composing room door. "Nick, *please*, we've got to have some decisions in here."

"Be right with you, Roz."

"That's what you promised twenty minutes ago," she said sourly, closing the door.

Nick turned to Annie, his expression curiously expectant. "Anything else I can do for you?"

"Nothing," she said, trying to force herself to look away but failing. "I've really got to rush. It's my day to work at the Senior Center. I'll take a few pictures while I'm there to make sure I understand all you've told me."

"Fine." He gestured for her to precede him through the door into the newsroom. He seemed to have gotten past their initial stiffness; would that she could do likewise! "Nice seeing you, Annie."

Nice seeing you, nice kissing you. Don't call me—I'll call you. Indignation pricked her, but ruthlessly she stamped it down. "Nice seeing you, too, Nick."

He moved toward the editors' island in the middle of the room. She spoke his name and he paused, looking back at her with brows arched.

"Thank you."

He seemed to consider for a moment. Then he shrugged. "Think nothing of it," he said.

She'd give anything if she could follow his advice.

ANNIE SHOT an entire roll of film at the Senior Citizens' Center. As luck would have it, she got one really terrific picture of Henrietta Kopeckne. The old lady was sitting in her wheelchair, surrounded by stuffed toys the senior citizens were making for children in a local program for disadvantaged kids. An uncharacteristic smile transformed the woman's usually stern features.

Of course, Annie didn't know how terrific the shot was when she took it. She found out when she opened the *Bandwagon* two days later and saw the photo on page one.

And a photo credit—they'd given her a photo credit! She couldn't believe it: *Bandwagon* Photo by Annie Page.

For the first time, she felt like a real professional. She hugged the paper to her chest and sat there in her kitchen, grinning foolishly, wondering whether she should give in to the desire to jump to her feet and dance around the room for joy.

This sense of fulfillment was unlike anything she'd ever experienced, even in her marriage. And she had Nick to thank for it. Nick... She sighed. He was on her mind entirely too much these days. Oh, but this was so like him, not even to tell her in advance about her first real success!

The telephone rang and she jumped, then reached for it and said a breathless "Hello?"

"Hello, Annie. This is Josephine Turnquist."

Annie felt so good even the councilman's snippy wife couldn't bring her down. "Yes, Josephine. What can I do for you?"

"I'm calling about the benefit dance for the new hospital wing. You know about it, of course—the Hospital HoeDown sponsored by the Women's Auxiliary?"

"Uh-huh." *Haven't you seen my photograph on the front page of the newspaper?* Annie wanted to shout. *Isn't it wonderful?* "Did you want me to buy a ticket or cover the event?" she asked instead.

"Both, actually."

"Sounds good." Annie reached for the pad of paper and pencil she'd started leaving near the telephone. "What're the details?"

"Next Saturday night, Western attire, eight o'clock at the country club."

Annie scribbled. "Got it. I'll be there."

"Good." Josephine's voice was heavy with satisfaction. "Oh, and the tickets are a hundred dollars. Each. If you bring a date, it's one-seventy-five. You can give us a check at the door.''

She hung up. Annie's heart stood still, then began to pound erratically. A hundred dollars! She didn't have that kind of money to spare, no matter how worthy the event. What was she going to do?

She was still wondering three hours later when she stopped at the newspaper office to drop off film. She'd come up with one idea—she could get sick Saturday and be unable to attend. Oh, but she didn't want to do that! It seemed so cowardly.

She was so engrossed in her own problems that she didn't watch where she was going. Rounding a corner, she plowed into a tall figure coming toward her. The instant she found herself breathless against the broad chest, she knew she'd run into Nick—literally. He caught her by the arms and helped her regain her balance.

''I'm sorry,'' she apologized, glancing up at him and then looking quickly away. But she'd seen his wide grin and her heart beat a little faster.

''Well?'' he urged.

''Well, what?''

''Well, how did you like finding your efforts on page one? I thought you'd be, if not ecstatic, at least mildly pleased to have a photo credit on the front page.''

He sounded so disappointed that she raised guilty eyes to his face. ''I was thrilled, really. I mean, I *am* thrilled.''

''You don't sound thrilled.'' He frowned. ''Out with it. What's wrong?''

''Nothing.'' She glanced down at her watch. ''I'm late for a meeting, Nick. I'd love to stay and chat but—'' She edged toward the door.

His expression hardened. ''No, you don't. You're not getting out of here until you tell me what's bothering you.''

"Nothing, really."

His implacable expression didn't soften. In fact, he looked more determined than ever. "My office. Now."

"But—" Robert would have accepted her excuses; why couldn't Nick? "Oh, all right," she gave in ungraciously. "If you insist."

She led the way, sitting down in the chair before his desk without invitation. He perched on one corner of the desk, resting a forearm on his thigh and contemplating her.

He seemed more concerned than angry. "Everything going all right?"

"Fine," she said too quickly.

He pursed his lips thoughtfully and the creases in his cheeks deepened—dimples, really. She realized she was staring and looked away hastily.

He leaned toward her, his head on a level with hers. "Your camera work's improving, obviously. Are you getting enough invitations to fill your column?"

She rolled her eyes. "More than enough."

"You don't have to accept everything that comes in the door," he reminded her. "You can pick and choose. Nothing's mandatory, except the big stuff—the Holiday Ball, the annual city picnic, stuff like that."

She nodded. That was a relief. Maybe she could just skip the—

"And this big hospital benefit coming up," he added.

Dismay flooded through her and she looked down, hoping he hadn't seen it in her face. How was she going to get out of attending now? With her vision lowered, she saw his foot begin to swing back and forth in an impatient rhythm.

"Okay, what's the problem?" he demanded. "I know Josephine Turnquist is involved in the auxiliary sponsoring the benefit, but surely that's not enough to keep you from going."

"No, of course not," she said, incensed he'd think such a thing.

"Then what is it? Come on, Annie, I don't have all day."

She twisted her fingers together and drew an agitated breath. For last week's column, she'd paid twenty-five dollars to attend the PTA fund-raiser, but the tea and the birthday party had been free. The newspaper was paying her a salary and mileage, for heaven's sake. How cheap could she get, whining about spending a few bucks on worthy causes?

He put his hands on her shoulders. It shocked her so much she jerked up her head and stared into his eyes.

"Tell me the truth. Why don't you want to cover this?"

The man never let up. She swallowed hard before answering. "In all honesty, Nick...in all honesty, I simply can't afford a hundred dollars...at this point...for a party."

That was just about the hardest thing she'd ever had to admit—that the supposedly wealthy widow *wasn't*. By the time she got to the end of the sentence she'd completely run out of steam. She drew a deep breath and looked up at him, prepared for the worst. But if he brought Robert's name into this, he'd regret it! she vowed.

The expression building on his face didn't encourage her. It seemed composed of equal parts disbelief and fury. His fingers clenched down painfully on her shoulders.

"Let me get this straight," he began, his voice measured and menacing despite its softness. "You're paying your own way to events you cover for this newspaper, and you're embarrassed because you don't have a hundred dollars lying around for some party?"

"Well, y-yes, that's about it." Once again she twisted her hands together, then realized what she was doing and forced herself to stop.

"Why?" He looked absolutely mystified. "Where did you get the harebrained idea that you should do that, anyway?"

"N-nobody told me otherwise," she said, trying not to sound defensive.

"Didn't you ever hear of common practices? It is *common practice* for employers to handle expenses necessary for employees to do the job they're hired for. I don't care if you've got more money than Queen Elizabeth." He released her abruptly and stood up. "Where the hell have you worked, woman?"

He raked his hand through his hair. She was relieved he wasn't so close to her anymore, but his height was almost equally intimidating.

"Nowhere," she admitted. "This is the first real job I've ever had." She rose and edged around until the chair stood between them. "Obviously, I'm a hopeless case. If you want my resignation, you have it."

Nick's head reared back, his expression astonished. "The woman's gone 'round the bend," he muttered. He pointed at the chair. "Sit down."

She backed away, feeling an unaccustomed stubbornness. "No, thanks. I don't—"

"Sit down!"

He meant business, that much was obvious. Determined as he was, it seemed unlikely she'd escape his wrath even if she sprinted for the door.

So she sat down, folded her hands in her lap and tried to compose her face. "I won't let you bully me," she said through trembling lips.

"I'm not—!" He gritted his teeth, his expression thunderous. He drew a deep breath. "Okay, I'm calm. See how calm I am?" The volume of his voice didn't decrease one iota as he went on. "Number one, stringers don't *resign*. They may quit, or they may get fired, but they'd not do anything nearly so grand as *resign*."

"I stand corrected." She spoke in a tight little voice. "If that's all—"

She started to rise and he stopped her with his hands on her shoulders. She was no match for him, she realized, no match at all.

He gritted his teeth. "I'm not even close to finished with you. Annie Page, you are the touchiest woman I ever ran into. Why do you get so flustered at every little mistake? I don't expect you to be perfect—hell, nobody's perfect." He glared at her. "Not even me."

"I never said I was perfect." *If he doesn't let me out of here, I'm going to fall apart completely.* She wasn't used to this kind of grilling and she didn't like it one little bit.

"I never said you said you— damn! You've got me so rattled I don't know what *anybody* said." He stamped around the desk and sat down. "You know what your problem is?"

"I wasn't aware until this very moment I *had* a problem."

"You do. Believe me, you do." He leaned forward, his elbows resting on the blotter. His anger had leveled off. "You're too thin-skinned. Shrinking violets don't survive in the news business."

"Oh, for heaven's sake." Now that his anger was abating, her own flared. "I've been called a lot of things in my time—"

"I know. Nice, hardworking, dedicated, dependable—"

"Wimpy, wishy-washy, goody-goody, shy—" Her glance clashed with his and she broke off the litany of her sins.

"Exactly," he said, looking satisfied. "A shrinking violet. You've got to get a handle on that or you'll give my profession a bad name. Newspaperpersons have to be tough, aggressive, determined." He smacked one fist into the opposite palm for emphasis.

"I believe you've just described yourself," she suggested cuttingly.

He arched his brows in mock surprise. "You may be right. But I wasn't always the hard-bitten newsman you see before you. I, too, was once a sensitive young journalist."

He was trying to jolly her out of her snit, she realized, and she wanted to resist such blatant manipulation. Still, he was skirting closer to personal revelation then she'd ever known him to do, and she was intrigued, as much as she tried not to show it. She knew nothing about this man, beyond his history in Buena Vista. In fact, he'd bought the *Bandwagon* only months before she and Robert moved to town.

"So how did this amazing transformation come about, sensitive young journalist to savvy reporter?" she asked, feeling herself tumble into his trap.

"The same way it'll happen to you. Through experience. I thought I was a real hotshot when I got my first foreign assignment—"

"A foreign correspondent?" Impressed despite herself, she began to relax a little.

He shrugged, making light of it. "Yeah. First time I got thrown in with the big boys I got my... ambition kicked. They made mincemeat out of me. I couldn't get a question in edgewise. Fortunately, a wise old reporter took me under his wing and made a man out of me, journalistically speaking. I'm offering to do the same for you."

"You mean you're offering to make a woman out of me?" The words popped out before she could stop them.

A dangerous glint appeared in his eyes. "Journalistically speaking, of course."

She felt the sudden flutter of her pulse and looked away. "M-my situation is quite different," she stammered.

"Not really. I had a lot to learn, you have a lot to learn. I was facing—as you're facing now—an unfamiliar situation. I had trouble asking questions because . . . the usual reasons, I suppose. I didn't want to look stupid, I didn't want to admit I didn't know it all, I didn't want anyone to realize I was a fraud."

"A fraud? You?" He was the most knowledgeable and self-assured man she'd ever known, although he wasn't generally obnoxious about it.

His look was wry. "Incredible but true. One thing I've never been, however, is thin-skinned, probably because I always had someone on hand to point out the errors of my ways."

As Annie had had: first her father and then Robert. She could sympathize with Nick. "Who was that?" she asked, her defenses crumbling before her genuine desire to learn more about this intriguing man.

He gave her a rueful smile.

"My wife," he said.

CHAPTER SEVEN

"YOU'RE *MARRIED*?" Dismay flooded through her. Somehow Nick and marriage seemed an incompatible combination.

"Once upon a time." He sounded defensive. "Hey, I was young. I wanted the whole enchilada—kids, a woman who'd meet me at the door wrapped in cellophane and ribbons, a dog to fetch my slippers."

"Is that what you got?" Her voice sounded muffled; she cleared her throat.

"If I had, I'd still be married," he said. "Or maybe not—who knows?"

"No kids, no dog?" She felt inexplicably better.

He shook his head. "No cellophane or ribbons, either. My wife made Attila the Hun look like a pussycat. Hell of a reporter, though. I worked for the *Times*, she worked for the *News*, and the first time we competed on a story she made a fool of me."

Annie couldn't imagine that. "So you got even," she suggested. "You married her." And she must have been the exact opposite of me, she added to herself.

"One of us got even." He grinned sheepishly. "I married her, she divorced me. That's on-the-job training the hard way. My point is, she toughened me up. I may not be a better man for the experience. I am a better journalist."

"But this is your profession," Annie protested. "I'm here by accident."

"So what? You *are* here, by fate or by design. Just remember that in this business, today's mistakes line tomorrow's bird cages. Both success and failure tend to be fleeting. Roll with the punches, keep trying, and you'll be all right."

"In other words," she interrupted, "don't be so thin-skinned." She rose and walked toward the door. She was already ten minutes late for a meeting.

Nick followed. "Think you can handle that?"

She hesitated. "I don't know. I'll try."

"Try, nothing." He put his hands on her shoulders and looked into her eyes. "You don't have to give my ex-wife a run for her money, but you do have to protect yourself. I'm saying this for your own good, Annie."

For your own good—a favorite platitude, first of her father's, then her husband's. How she hated that expression, no matter how sincerely offered.

"Please don't patronize me," she said through tight lips, surprised to hear herself speaking up. Something about Nick just brought out the worst in her. "I can take care of myself." She stepped away from the implied control of his light grip.

He stared at her as if he feared she'd lost her mind. Then his brows lowered and he let out his breath in a hiss of exasperation. "Famous last words. Be careful they don't come back to haunt you." Whipping around, he stalked to his desk.

Annie bit her lip. Should she apologize? Good manners required it, she decided. "Nick," she began hesitantly, "I—"

In the act of drawing out his chair, he straightened, pinning her with his slashing gaze. "Turn in receipts for all work-related expenses and you'll be reimbursed," he said crisply. "That'll be all."

He sat down and reached for a stack of files. She'd been dismissed.

NICK WAS NOT ONE to carry a grudge, Annie soon discovered to her vast surprise. The next time she saw him—at a Chamber of Commerce breakfast for new members—he treated her as if nothing had happened.

Again.

He had kissed her and forgotten about it; he'd chewed her out and forgotten about it just as quickly. Yet he'd managed to sustain the quarrel with Robert for years. It simply didn't make sense.

Or maybe it did.

What if it did? Annie froze, a forkful of French toast halfway to her mouth. Her astonished eyes met Nick's blue gaze across the table. He nodded in that solemn way he had, the one that warned her that laughter lay just beneath the surface.

Maybe Robert really *didn't* know how to play the game. Maybe he had never learned that Nick had his own job to do, which sometimes put him at odds with the bureaucracy and, potentially, everybody else.

Or maybe Robert knew and didn't care.

"Could you pass that carafe of coffee, Annie?"

With a start, she realized she'd forgotten where she was. "I'm sorry—of course." She passed the plastic container to Sheila Eastman, owner of Sheila's Very Unique Fashions.

Sheila smiled her thanks. "Say, Annie," she remarked casually, "I've been reading the Society Page in the *Bandwagon* and it's wonderful since you took over. It occurs to me . . ."

"Yes?" Annie offered polite encouragement. She didn't know Sheila very well, since the woman didn't go in much for civic endeavors or volunteer work. They were about the same age, however.

"I have a fashion show coming up in a couple of weeks." Sheila refilled her cup and Annie's as well. "I'll be showing some very unique garments. It would make a wonderful item for your column. You're such a wonderful writer—I don't know how you do it."

"I appreciate the kind words," Annie said, trying not to bask too obviously in the praise. "To tell you the truth, I'm still learning." She stirred sugar into her coffee. "A fashion show . . . I haven't covered one of those yet."

"I can promise you a good time. There'll be champagne and wonderful food and—"

"Yo, Kimball!"

Sheila was interrupted by a man at the end of the table. He leaned forward, a challenging smile on his florid face. "I didn't much like that editorial on the front page the other day," he blustered.

"Who *is* that?" Sheila whispered.

"I don't remember his name," Annie replied in a low voice. "I think he's the new owner of the service station on Hacienda Drive." She—and the other twenty or so people in the room—followed the man's gaze to the opposite side of the table.

Nick, in the middle of a conversation with Mitch Priddy, turned slowly toward the offending speaker. "We don't run editorials on the front page," he said in a tone that dismissed the man and his complaint as inconsequential. "That's where we put the news."

The man's face flushed even redder. "You know what I mean," he insisted. "That edi-story about downtown revitalization. I don't know who that reporter talked to but he sure didn't come to me. I'd have told him—"

"Feel free to do so," Nick interrupted. "His name's Curtis Harvey and you can reach him at 555-5146, extension 27."

Nick shifted around in his chair and resumed his conversation with Mitch, quelling the red-faced man without ever raising his voice.

Annie felt a cold chill race down her spine. Easy for Nick to tell her to "be tough." He didn't have to face himself.

At that moment he glanced up and their eyes met. He gave her a wink and a smile so intimate—and so quickly gone—she thought she'd imagined them. All her apprehension fled. He really *was* a nice guy, she suddenly acknowledged.

SHEILA'S FASHION SHOW turned out to be quite ordinary, but the retired teachers' picnic and the community theater opening more than made up for it. Annie's confidence soared to new heights.

I'm really getting the hang of this, she congratulated herself—just as she bumped the back cover release of her camera and exposed all the film from the picnic.

Quaking in her shoes, she went upstairs to the *Bandwagon* to confess her blunder to Nick.

"He's in the morgue," the harried receptionist said in response to Annie's query.

Annie's jaw dropped, along with her stomach. "Did someone die?"

The receptionist laughed. "Not yet, but the day's not over." She ignored three incoming telephone calls to point toward the stairs. "The morgue's up there, Annie. It's where they keep the old newspaper clippings and files. Yesterday's news, so to speak—dead stuff. The morgue . . . get it?"

Annie got it. She was so relieved that nothing had happened to Nick that she ran up the stairs two at a time and burst in on him. He stood in front of a row of cabinets, rummaging through a file drawer. He glanced up with a frown, but when he saw her he smiled.

"Where's the fire?" he asked.

Annie skidded to a halt, her pleasure at seeing him both tangible and bewildering. In the musty confines of the little room, his powerful physical presence threatened to overwhelm her.

He'd taken off his tie and opened the top button of his pale blue shirt. She fancied she could see the throb of his pulse at the base of his strong brown throat. She swallowed hard.

He cocked his head to one side. "Annie? What's the matter?"

"I think I'm still reacting to the word *morgue*," she said, sparing a glance around. The loss of the film now seemed a paltry thing. She'd take her lumps and be tough about it. She gave him a smile completely open and genuine. "I'm here to confess," she said almost cheerfully. "I goofed."

He slid the heavy drawer closed without looking down, mashing several files in the process. His dark brows rose. "I can hardly wait to hear how."

"I accidentally ruined the roll of film I shot at the teachers' picnic. I'll never do it again, I swear." She sighed. "Of course, I'll probably come up with something just as bad. So go ahead—yell at me. I promise I'll take it like a man."

She hammed playfully, screwing up her face and hunching her shoulders in preparation for any verbal blows he might hurl at her.

"I don't want to yell at you. And I sure as hell don't want you taking anything like a man. We'll just make the other pictures bigger."

He walked toward her until he was close enough to reach out and touch her forearms lightly. Caught off guard, she stared at him, breathing suspended.

He slid his hands down her arms, encircling her wrists lightly, his thumbs massaging her pulse points. "Let's go somewhere and talk about this," he suggested in a low voice. "How about dinner?"

She wanted to. Oh, how she wanted to! But the very strength of her desire to give in warned her that she must be strong. "I'm sorry," she said, pulling away from him. She rubbed her wrists, where his hands had rested. "I can't."

She could see him pull back into himself, becoming again the boss instead of the man.

"You mean you don't want to," he said.

"It's the same thing, in polite circles." She took a step away from him, toward the door. "I am sorry," she said in a rush. "I don't like to disappoint you. If it's any consolation, I'm more disappointed in myself than you could ever be."

"Are we talking about film or dinner?"

At that moment, she couldn't have said.

ANNIE LAY IN BED Sunday morning, trying to catch up on the sleep she'd missed the night before. First she'd attended a community craft fair and then she'd gone to the hospital benefit, which wasn't much fun, once she realized Nick wasn't going to show up.

Not that she'd wanted to see him, she assured herself righteously, crawling out of bed. She'd just been curious to see if he'd bring a date. That possibility brought a twinge to her midsection.

As she reached for a light summer robe, a horrendous pounding commenced on her front door.

Her first thought was that something had happened to Lew. Her stomach lurched. This could only be bad news, and the only person she had left to get bad news about was her stepson. Just last week he'd reported his leg healing nicely, but something must have happened.

Without waiting to find her slippers, Annie ran barefoot down the hall and threw open the door. Nicholas Kimball stood there, one hand fisted to bang against the door and the other crumpling a newspaper. His fierce expression would have given pause to a band of marauding terrorists.

"What's the meaning of this?" he shouted, thrusting the paper in her astonished face. "You've devoted half a page to society simps—we've been had by nonadvertisers! What're you trying to do, make us all look like morons?"

He strode inside and she fell back before his unexpected attack. She stared at him, her breathing ragged with fright. Unconsciously she tightened the belt on her robe. "I . . . we . . . it just . . ."

He intimidated her, despite her best efforts to the contrary. He looked so big and bold and sure in his rage. Even his sleek denim trousers and the white cotton sweater he wore made him seem darker and more dangerous than usual. And more attractive.

"Well?" he demanded. "Are you just going to stand there and take it? Don't you have anything to say for yourself?"

"Yes!" The anger behind that one word surprised her as much as it must have surprised him. She balled her hands into fists and took a step—not away, but toward him. "I mean no. I mean no, I told you I messed up that film, you big bully."

Her voice trembled; confrontations of any sort were completely foreign to her nature. She never lost her cool that way—never.

"I'm talking about what's *on* this page, not what isn't." He whacked the paper against his thigh for emphasis. "You should have told Sheila to buy an ad, if she wanted space in the paper."

Annie frowned. "That's what you're mad about?"

"Sheila Eastman is an opportunist who takes every advantage she can. She hasn't spent a penny advertising in the *Bandwagon* since she went into business, and she never misses a chance to put the rap on us in public. But when she can find a way to wangle free advertising, she's right there."

"Oh!" Annie clapped one hand over her mouth in horror. "Why didn't you *tell* me? You saw me sitting next to her at that Chamber of Commerce breakfast."

"I thought you knew. I thought *everybody* knew." He threw her a disgusted glance. "Where the hell were Debbie and Roz while all this was going on?" He gritted his teeth. "Maybe I'm yelling at the wrong—"

"Don't you dare start on them! It's my mistake and I'll take the consequences." She squared her shoulders and tried to meet his outraged glance, efforts complicated by her struggle to hold back tears.

"Damn, Annie, are you going to cry?" He shoved his hand through his hair, his forehead wrinkling with consternation. "I can't stand it when women cry."

"I'm not crying, nor do I intend to," she choked, blinking rapidly. She shoved the long tangle of hair away from her face with both hands, wishing she wasn't facing him barefoot in her bathrobe, still warm from her bed. She felt defenseless in this state of dishabille.

"Thank God." He heaved a great sigh, which seemed to calm him. "Look, I'm a reasonable man. I'm prepared to accept ignorance as a defense. Let's call a truce. I got so excited I came over here without even a cup of coffee. Any chance you could offer me one?"

"You're joking! You barge in here yelling at me—" As she spoke, she turned toward the kitchen, her back straight and unyielding even as she yielded.

"I didn't start the yelling, you did. I was calm and controlled."

He followed her, draping his tall frame over a stool at the breakfast bar. She ignored him, pulling the can of coffee from the freezer, taking a paper filter from a drawer. She needed this respite to pull her shattered nerves together.

He watched her, his expression perplexed. "Did you mean what you said back there, that I act like a bully?" he demanded suddenly.

Astonishment got the better of her and she risked a glance at him, the first since they'd entered the kitchen. He looked like anything *but* a bully at the moment, with that puzzled expression on his face. As always when he let his vulnerable side peek through, she felt her resolve weaken. *Hold your ground,* she warned herself. *Take his advice and be tough.*

"I didn't say you acted that way, I said you *are* that way." She poured water into the coffee machine and switched it on. "It's very intimidating to a person taught to respect authority."

She saw his surprise, and in truth she was surprised herself. She didn't go around making personally revealing comments, as a general rule.

Once again she fumbled unconsciously at the belt of her robe, shuffling her bare feet. "If you're going to stay for coffee, I'd better get dressed."

"No, sit down." He patted the stool next to his. "Coffee'll be ready soon and then we can talk."

"I'm not sure I want to talk," she said, but that wasn't entirely true. She wanted very much to get back to that easy, comfortable feeling they sometimes shared. She slipped onto the stool and took a deep breath. "I'm really sorry," she murmured, not looking at him. "I honestly didn't understand."

"Yeah, well, I may have overreacted." He shifted uncomfortably. "I guess we never spelled it out. If the proceeds had gone to a worthy cause..."

At his questioning look, she shook her head. "Proceeds went to Sheila's Very Unique Fashions."

"In that case, she should have bought an ad. The woman's a real con artist. It's standard operating procedure with her, suckering in the new reporters. Someone—no—*I* should have warned you." He shrugged. "If there'd been any altruistic angle at all..."

"I see." She looked down at her hands, twisting together restlessly in her lap. "I should have figured that out. I can't blame you for being mad." She darted him an anxious glance. "Are you mad I said that?"

"You must think I'm a complete jerk to even ask," he growled. "In my family, if you didn't yell nobody paid any attention to you. Your family, I'd venture to guess, was different."

"Oh, yes."

"What did your father do, Annie?"

All his attention centered on her as if at that moment she were the most important person in his world. She felt a glow of pleasure begin in the pit of her stomach and spread, until it eased the nervous tightness in her chest.

"He was a career Army officer. I'm an Army brat." Her voice was barely a whisper. "When people hear that, they think I must have lived in lots of exciting and exotic places, but I didn't."

"Why not?"

She shrugged. She didn't like talking about her family, but for some reason, she found herself answering his questions. "My mother was . . . sick a lot."

"Sick?" He picked up on the slight hesitation right away.

Even now, after all these years, she felt guilty giving an honest reply. "That was our family euphemism for alcoholism. My mother was an alcoholic."

"That's tough." He looked as if he really understood. "You're an only child?" Could that gentle voice belong to the same man who'd stormed in here minutes before?

Annie nodded. "When my father went overseas, he'd leave my mother and me wherever we happened to be. We did accompany him on one tour of duty in Germany when I was about twelve. But it wasn't any different—we might as well have been in America. We were rarely off the post." She hesitated. "I never felt I really belonged anywhere, until Buena Vista."

She jumped up off her stool. "Coffee's ready," she said brightly, bustling around to pour it.

"Your father was strict, I take it," Nick said in a neutral tone.

"Yes." Annie set a steaming mug before him. "Sugar? Milk?"

He shook his head.

"Toast? I don't have any rolls or doughnuts but—"

He reached across the breakfast bar and caught her agitated hands in his. Their gazes locked, hers flustered, his compassionate. She should pull away but somehow she couldn't. He held her still for a moment, and she felt the tension and strain drain away, to be replaced by something warmer and infinitely more alarming.

"I didn't come for breakfast," he said. "I came...I don't know why I came. I thought it was to yell at you, but maybe I came because you turned me down the other day when you found me in the morgue."

Insecurity in Nick Kimball's voice? She couldn't believe it.

"Hey, don't stare at me as if you'd just found out I tear wings off butterflies," he said in a testy tone. "I'm only human."

He looked wonderfully human at the moment, his dark hair tousled and his lean face unguarded. She felt herself respond, even to the point of leaning toward him.

"Come sit down," he ordered. "Relax, drink your coffee, tell me about Annie Page."

She melted. She had always considered blue eyes cold, but she knew now how wrong she'd been. And if she could be wrong about blue eyes, what else might she be wrong about?

They sat on the big floral couch in the family room and talked. And talked...

Her father was strict, but she wasn't a rebellious child so that was rarely an issue, she told Nick.

"I didn't have time to rebel," she said matter-of-factly, "what with school and taking care of Mother. My senior year, she. .took a turn for the worse. I wanted to go on to college, and I did register and attend for a few months... "

Over her father's objections. He'd been coldly disapproving— "When the going gets rough, people tend to bail out on you," she'd told Nick upon another occasion. Her mini-rebellion didn't last long. Her mother, in a bout of drunkenness, had tripped and fallen down a flight of stairs. Annie had had no choice except to withdraw from college and take care of the bedridden woman.

But what she said to Nick was, "I eventually dropped out of college."

"How did you meet Robert?" Nick asked. "Army, Marines, and never the twain shall mix, I thought."

"Usually. Not always." Annie twined her fingers through the handle of her mug. "My father was stationed at Fort Sam Houston in San Antonio—Fort Sam, it's called. Robert was on recruiting duty for the Corps. I don't know how they actually met but my father brought him home for dinner one night."

"How long ago was that?"

She shrugged. "I don't know. I was twenty-two and now I'm thirty-five. Thirteen years, I guess."

"How old was Robert?"

It was said too casually, and she darted him a suspicious glance. "Older," she replied firmly. Actually, Robert had been thirty-eight, but she saw no reason to tell Nick that. "And Lew was eight."

Her voice softened when she said her stepson's name. Lew was the real attraction at first. He'd been a handful—not a bad boy, just mischievous. His mother had died three years earlier and he'd been shunted around to a series of day-care centers and baby-sitters. It showed. He desperately needed love.

And Annie desperately longed to give love.

Nick turned his coffee mug around in his hands. "I suppose you and Robert were married before he got orders out of San Antonio."

"That's close." Actually, when Robert got orders to Japan he proposed that she marry him and stay behind in Texas with his son. It seemed a perfect solution. She admired and respected Robert and thought she understood him. And she adored Lew, who was beginning to respond to her.

The year Robert was gone, she and Lew had lived with her parents, and she'd cared for her mother as well as her stepson. Her mother died a few months before Robert returned to take his family to his next duty station at Twentynine Palms, in the California desert. Her father died two years later.

"It was pleasant enough at Twentynine Palms," she told Nick. "I was active in the Officers' Wives Club, volunteered with the Red Cross and Navy Relief, did a lot of entertaining and in general tried to make myself useful."

"And eventually you came here."

"Yes," she said. "Eventually we came here."

And everybody knew what had happened then.

"It begins to make sense," Nick said slowly, "your respect for authority. Annie, the *Bandwagon* isn't the Army and it isn't the Marine Corps. You're allowed to disagree with me." His grin flashed. "But not too often."

She leaned back in her corner of the couch, feeling lightheaded with relief at unburdening herself. Saying the words out loud helped her come to grips with fears and feelings she'd long suppressed. She hadn't realized how much she trusted Nick, until all—or almost all—her secrets had come pouring out.

Now she even felt comfortable joking with him. "When I disagree, I suppose it should be at the top of my lungs or you won't notice," she suggested.

He laughed. "That's right. You can do it, too. Hell, my mother was no bigger than you are and she handled three boys and one husband with no problem."

"I'll bet she had her hands full, whether you knew it or not," Annie guessed. "Was your father a journalist?"

"Lawyer. He worked for the Justice Department in Washington, D.C. My mother was the journalist. Between babies and family emergencies, she worked as a lifestyles reporter, or in features, as they called it then. She was one tough cookie—she wanted to be a political reporter, but back in the old days that wasn't possible for women with so many family responsibilities, even with perseverance. She never complained, just did the best she could and didn't belabor the fact that she'd never make it onto the fast track."

"And you got your love for newspapering from her."

He nodded. "That, and my love...my respect for women who do the best they can without dwelling on what might have been."

He took her cup from her hand, its contents cold and unappealing, and set it on the floor. Her hand lay in his, vulnerable and trembling. For a moment he stared down at it and then his thumb curved to stroke the tender contours. Her fingers tightened convulsively and her wide-eyed gaze flew to his face.

He smiled, the corners of his eyes crinkling. Dimples deepened in his cheeks. "You know," he said thoughtfully, "I really didn't like you. Roz had to practically hold a pistol to my head to get me to offer you the job."

"Offer?" Annie's laugh came out weak and breathless. "If that was an offer, it was a very *strong* one."

His eyes sparkled. "Okay, okay, you got me there." His expression sobered. "While we're being painfully honest with each other, I'll also admit to taking a certain pleasure in quarreling with your husband."

This revelation seemed to weigh heavily upon him, and he looked down at their joined hands. "I was sorry when he died," he said gruffly. "I mean that, Annie. Everyone needs loyal opposition and he was mine."

She chewed on her lower lip, her thoughts in turmoil. She hadn't liked Nick, either...before. Or had she been trying to deny an attraction she felt even then? The quarrel between the two men would have made that possible. Stunned, she admitted to herself that Nick Kimball affected her as no man ever had.

No other man. Including Robert.

Nick cupped her chin with gentle fingers. "What is it?" he asked, his tone anxious. "Have I hurt your feelings again?"

She shook her head. "It's not that." What was she thinking? She had been Robert's wife. She owed him unwavering loyalty. "It's what you said about taking pleasure in the quarrel." She looked at Nick, searching for answers she didn't expect to find. "Do you think Robert felt the same way?"

Nick frowned. "Sure. Otherwise we'd have made peace long ago. It takes two to tango and at least two to wage war."

Had the fault been as much Robert's as Nick's? No! That thought was unworthy of her. She'd been raised to believe that nothing was more important than loyalty—loyalty to country and to family, and certainly to the man she married—sometimes blind loyalty.

She spoke her thoughts out loud. "He wasn't like that. It would trivialize all he stood for to make a game out of it. His memory is very important to me and always will be."

She moved away from Nick's touch. Although she longed to feel his arms around her, she didn't dare succumb to that temptation. Desire, clean and pure and simple, coiled through her like a tightening spring ... and he saw it. He captured her hand and drew it up to brush her sensitized palm against the curve of his jaw.

She caught her breath, reveling in the smooth texture of his skin. Her fingers arched, the soft tips pressing against the strong contours of his face. If she moved her thumb the tiniest bit, it would brush across his lips, his mustache. All her resistance evaporated, replaced by a storm of confusion.

"Forget Robert," he said in a voice that vibrated from deep inside his chest. "I'll help you...."

CHAPTER EIGHT

"YOU DON'T KNOW what you're suggesting," Annie blurted angrily. "Surely you realize I'll never—"

"Never say never."

Nick leaned closer. For just an instant she lost herself in clear blue eyes fringed by lush dark lashes and then his mouth touched hers, at once tender and fiery. With the sight of him suddenly too powerful to bear, her eyelids fluttered down.

She had waited for this, longed for this, consciously or unconsciously. Unable to stop herself, she curled her arms around his neck, clinging with all the strength she possessed. He urged her mouth open, and she felt a bolt of lightning shafting through her. An unfamiliar heat curled in the pit of her stomach.

This was what she had dreamed of as a young girl and never found, this welter of emotion. Restlessly she twisted her fingers through the thick dark hair at the nape of his neck as desire, in its intensity, ripped through her.

This couldn't be happening, not to ladylike Annie Page, Buena Vista's Citizen of the Year. She had gone to her husband a virgin on her wedding night, and he had taken her gently, setting a standard from which he never varied. His lovemaking had remained quick and almost... respectful, to the very end.

Robert had never aroused her to this fever pitch, not even at the moment of joining. If Nick could set her on fire with a kiss, what might he do if— No, she couldn't think about that, mustn't anticipate what could never be. Where was her fabled self-control when she most needed it?

He lifted his mouth from hers to lavish kisses across her cheek, her closed eyelids, her temple. "Annie," he groaned, the sensuous brush of his mustache making her shiver. "Let's start over."

Dazed and disoriented, she opened her eyes. She was surprised to find herself half-reclining on the arm of the couch, Nick leaning above her. She felt his thigh against hers and realized with alarm that her robe had parted, exposing her bare legs.

"Start over?" she repeated in confusion.

"This day. Our... relationship, whatever that is." He planted a quick, hard kiss on her lips and sat up. "I mean from the beginning—from the first time we ever laid eyes on each other, before all the hard feelings and bad blood."

He took her hands and pulled her up beside him. "I've never known anyone like you, Annie," he said, his tone and expression perplexed. "I thought you were as one-dimensional as a paper doll, but I was wrong. I've seen so many sides to you—the society matron, the hardworking columnist, the loyal wife, the dedicated mother, the doer of good deeds. I guess my cynical nature hasn't figured out which is the real Annie Page."

She gave a nervous little laugh and smoothed her robe over her knees. Her lips felt swollen and tender from his kisses and her agitated breathing still hadn't settled down. "You make it sound so complicated, Nick. I'm really quite simple. What you see is what you get."

"I wish." His closed expression lightened and she saw a spark of excitement begin to build in his eyes. "Let's find out. Spend the day with me."

"Doing what?" The day—a whole day? Did she dare? *Forgive me for considering it, Robert,* she apologized silently.

Nick gestured expansively with widespread arms. "Whatever you want. Sky's the limit."

She shook her head. "I can't. I volunteered to work at a tea dance this afternoon at the Senior Citizens' Center." Would she have had the strength to refuse him otherwise? she wondered. "I thought I could also use the item for the column," she added as a clincher.

She was getting a grip on herself again. She leaned down and picked up the coffee mugs from the floor. Rising, she carried them toward the breakfast bar separating the family room from the kitchen. Even though he no longer touched her, she still tingled with the memory of him. "Then at four," she continued, "there's an ice cream social to benefit the youth soccer league—also for the column and also strictly legitimate."

"I wouldn't suggest otherwise." He looked offended.

She started to rinse the mugs, but his frown caused her to hesitate. "Would you like more coffee?" she asked, disgusted with the hopeful note she heard in her voice.

"Please." When she set his refilled mug on the counter before him, he said too casually, "Maybe I'll let you talk me into going with you. I like to show the flag at local events, once in a while."

"Show the flag?"

He shrugged. "Be seen. Maintain a presence. It's the Teddy Roosevelt approach to public relations."

Her laughter offered mere lip service. She wanted him to stay; she wanted him to go; she wanted him to go with her. She wanted to be able to think straight. "I don't know if that's a good idea," she said finally.

What would it be like to spend an entire day with Nick Kimball?

Probably quite wonderful. Certainly quite dangerous.

He was watching her with close attention. He lifted his mug and held it between capable hands, but didn't drink. "You don't trust me," he stated accusingly. "Even now, after that—"

He broke off and gestured with a flick of his head toward the couch behind him, the couch where they'd come together so explosively. "If I had wanted a cheap affair..."

He didn't have to finish that statement. He had pulled back, not she. He could have taken her right there in her husband's home. She would have hated herself afterward, but at the moment she'd been powerless to resist.

He must have recognized her dismay. "Don't be afraid," he said gently. "I wouldn't do that to you. I'm not the monster I've been made out to be."

She *was* afraid, she admitted to herself. She knew full well that nothing could possibly come of any relationship between them and yet ... why shouldn't she have this one day to remember?

"Well?" he prodded. "Do you want company this afternoon?"

If she said no, he'd leave, she saw it in his eyes. The decision was hers alone. "Yes," she said, before she could change her mind. "I guess I do."

His brows rose and a tiny smile hovered around his lips. "In that case, go put yourself together and don't worry about me. I'll read the Sunday papers. Go on, now."

She went, feeling light-headed and years younger. Funny, last time she'd fancied herself in love she'd felt years older. *Stop it, Annie,* she cautioned herself. *Nobody mentioned love.*

ANNIE PICKED UP the tray of tiny cucumber and cream cheese sandwiches and carried it through the kitchen door. All the furniture in the senior citizens' game room had been pushed back against the walls to make room for dancing. Sammy and His Swinging Seniors provided musical accompaniment for couples twirling around the floor.

Nick swooped past, holding eighty-six-year-old Edna Peck lightly in his arms. Across her snowy head, his glance met Annie's and he winked. She grinned back at him; her face was stiff from so many smiles, she realized as she moved toward the refreshment table.

Mrs. Kopeckne sat in her wheelchair, next to the punch bowl. She did not look happy.

"May I fix you a plate, Mrs. Kopeckne?" Annie asked as she set the tray down. "These little sandwiches are wonderful."

"No, thank you, dear. My son is coming by later, and I don't want to be sitting here with a lap full of food when he arrives."

Annie sighed. Henrietta Kopeckne seemed to spend her life waiting for a son who never appeared. But maybe this time he really would show up. Annie hoped so.

The music—if the sound issuing from an accordian, a violin and drums could be so labeled—wallowed to a conclusion. On the dance floor, Nick gave Edna a courtly bow before leading her toward the punch bowl.

Edna was almost the exact opposite of Henrietta. Small and sprightly, she looked up at her tall escort, her eyes twinkling. "If I was only fifty years younger!" she declared. "Thanks for the dance, good lookin'."

Nick gave her a smile and then turned to Annie, his expression devilish. "I think I'm about danced out. Could I interest you in a stroll through the gardens?"

"I'm supposed to be working," she said, wincing at how pious she sounded.

"Harrumph!" Edna planted her hands on her hips and cocked her head to one side. "Get your fanny out of here, girl, before this fine-lookin' man realizes there's other fish in the sea." She gave Annie a shove that was none too gentle. "Get along with you, now."

Nick's hand on Annie's elbow sent little tremors of excitement streaking up her arm as he steered her toward the door. Behind them trailed Henrietta's complaining voice. "I wish you wouldn't butt in, Edna. You've got no more manners than a calico cat. Thank heaven William wasn't here to see that."

And Edna's laughing answer, "Put a stopper in it, Henry. You spend too much time worrying about William."

Outside, Nick and Annie settled onto a wrought-iron bench nestled beneath the trailing branches of a pepper tree.

Nick leaned back, his long legs outstretched and his face pensive. "This has been a real eye-opener," he remarked, watching the aged but often agile dancers through the floor-to-ceiling windows. "I should get out in the community more often." He slanted her a warmly approving glance. "Have you been volunteering here long?"

"Since we came to Buena Vista." She twisted her fingers together in her lap. "About five years, I guess."

He looked up into the branches of the tree, and she studied his strong profile. She was beginning to appreciate the very boldness that had unnerved her before she got to know him—if indeed she *did* know him now.

He tilted his head toward her. Sunlight filtered through the lacy leaves, casting intriguing patterns on his dark face. She longed to reach out and trail her fingers along his cheek, explore the dimpled creases.... His voice interrupted her erotic thoughts. "Did Robert join you in good deeds?"

She stiffened at the mention of Robert. "He didn't really have time. Lew helped quite often."

Nick reached up and snapped a twig from the branch overhead. "Your husband wasn't an easy man to please. Must have been tough, to be his son."

"That's true of many fathers and sons," she said defensively.

Nick turned toward her on the bench, still holding the pepper tree twig. Before she knew what he was doing, he brushed the delicate leaves across her mouth. Her lips parted in astonishment and she stared at him, mesmerized by her sensual response.

She should stand up and walk away. This was dangerous. Someone might see them. Someone—

Nick dropped the twig and reached out to slide one hand around the back of her neck, beneath the silky strands of her hair. His wrist and forearm were a heavy, comforting weight on her shoulder.

"I don't want to talk about Robert or Lew or the price of tea in China," he said, his voice husky.

"N-neither do I," she admitted as his fingers tightened on the stiff muscles of her neck. Aroused, she wanted to close her eyes and stretch like a cat. "I don't think I want to talk at all."

His teeth, beneath the dark shadow of his mustache, were a blur of brilliant white. "My sentiments exactly."

What she meant was that she didn't want to talk because she felt obliged to remove herself from his disturbing presence, but he didn't give her a chance to explain. Instead he drew her towards him. With his free hand, he stroked her cheek, his thumb exploring the soft curves.

She lifted her hands to his chest, intending to push him away. She must tell him to stop, that they were public people leading public lives. She, for one, valued her good reputation.

"Nick," she said in warning, but her ragged voice lacked conviction. She dug her fingers into taut muscle. "Nick, I—"

"Shhh." He held her chin still with his fingers and brushed his lips over hers, increasing her torment. "You don't have to say anything. I know."

She had no idea what he might know, but felt comforted by his assurances anyway. With a sigh that whispered of surrender, she swayed toward him, her lips parting to welcome his kiss—just as the back door of the Senior Center slammed open.

"I know they're out here someplace," Henrietta insisted, her voice querulous.

"Well if they are, we should have the good grace to leave 'em alone," was Edna's tart reply.

Annie bolted out of Nick's arms and onto her feet as if propelled by an unseen force. Trembling, she looked down at him. "I-I'd better get back inside and take a few pictures before everybody goes home," she stammered.

"What's your problem, lady?" He looked up at her with turbulent eyes, a deep furrow appearing between his brows.

"Isn't it obvious? This is hardly the time or place for—" she glanced guiltily at the bench "—for that sort of thing." She turned away.

"*That* sort of thing?" He shook his head as if he didn't believe his ears. "Look, Annie, I'm trying to be understanding, here, but you're not making it easy."

For a moment their eyes locked. Then she turned and walked away, her back straight and her thoughts askew.

"AND I TOLD RONNIE, hey, relax! Only your barber knows for sure. There's no *way* they can prove you dye your hair."

Annie, leaning back in the passenger seat of Nick's BMW, choked with laughter. "You mean to tell me you're on a first-name basis with—?"

"Kings, presidents, rock stars and charlatans. Some fit into more than one category."

"And you left that glamorous life for a little old one-horse town like Buena Vista?"

Nick made a left turn. "Surprises me sometimes, too. But at the time, I was suffering from severe burnout. When my grandmother died and left me and my brothers a bundle of cash, I figured what the hell? Most journalists dream of owning a newspaper and I was no exception. I had a chance to make that dream come true."

"Has it?"

"Yes. I don't regret a thing." He glanced around as the car glided down the main business thoroughfare. "I just realized I don't know where I'm going. Is this shindig being held at the soccer fields?"

Annie nodded. His declaration distracted her: *I don't regret a thing.* Must be nice, she thought. She regretted plenty, not the least of which was the way she overreacted every time he touched her.

He, on the other hand, seemed unaffected by the episode beneath the pepper tree. He'd sauntered back inside the Center as if nothing at all had happened. Then he'd proceeded to charm her with stories and anecdotes and small attentions that brought her as much pleasure as his arms and lips had earlier.

Almost as much pleasure, she added as a concession to honesty.

The ice cream social was well underway when they arrived, and it seemed as if everyone attending the soccer fund-raiser knew either Nick or Annie or both. At least half of them looked astonished to see the two together; the other half seemed astonished to see Nick, period. And all of them radiated curiosity.

"Don't worry about it," Nick advised during the lull in the procession of the sincere, the curious and the opportunistic. "They'll lose interest and go away as soon as the ice cream's ready."

"I hope," she said fervently.

Nick left her sitting on a wooden bench in the shade while he went to stand in line for ice cream. Almost immediately, Sheila Eastman materialized.

"Wonderful write-up on the fashion show," Sheila gushed. "Your column today was the best ever."

Annie didn't let her disgruntled feelings show. No point in making an issue of it, she instructed herself. "Thank you," she said.

"There'll be another show in a few months and I'll give you the exclusive," Sheila continued confidently.

"We'll see," Annie replied vaguely. She stood up. "If you'll excuse me—"

"I can count on you, then?" Sheila pressed for a commitment. "I'll even introduce you as a VIP."

Annie stood up. "That's very thoughtful but I'll have to pass."

Sheila frowned. "How disappointing. Tell you what, I'll arrange a nice little discount for you at my store while you think it over."

Dumbstruck, Annie sat back down on the bench, hard. Incredible, and yet one glance at Sheila's self-assured face and Annie knew this was no joke.

"Sheila Eastman, I didn't hear that," Annie declared. "You took advantage of me once and I got in trouble for it. I'm not going to make the same mistake twice."

Sheila's steady smile never wavered. "I guess I know how you got out of trouble." She glanced toward the ice cream tables, just as Nick turned around with dishes in both hands

"What are you implying?" Annie gasped.

"Oh, Annie, don't be such a prig," Sheila said, her tone mock-teasing. "Everyone in town knows you've got a thing going with Nicky. Gosh, why would he be here otherwise?"

"I *work* for the man!"

"Of course you do." Sheila bent forward and whispered in Annie's ear. "Hey, if Robert's opinion couldn't stop you, surely you're not worried about the people in this town! I just thought if you've loosened up enough to consort with the enemy, you might be willing to bend the rules a little for me, too. No hard feelings, okay?" She left with a cheery wave of one hand.

In shock, Annie sat as if rooted to the bench. Nick walked up and offered her a dish of ice cream.

"I got you vanilla," he announced. "You look like a vanilla sort of person to me." He glanced down at his own serving and frowned. "I got myself chocolate. There's doubtless a message here someplace."

Annie looked at the melting white slush in her bowl and felt her spirits dissolving along with the ice cream. So the whole town was talking, was it? She looked up at Nick with a kind of desperation. "Trade you." She held out her bowl. "I'm sick and tired of being a vanilla sort of person."

Nick looked surprised but readily exchanged his dish of ice cream for hers. "You're the boss," he said.

And the way he said it sent a little chill down her spine. He had made the right decision for them both earlier, but from here on out she'd have to be strong.

The ice cream, made in old-fashioned crank freezers, tasted creamy and delicious. Annie didn't even object when Nick sneaked a spoonful of chocolate. In truth, she enjoyed sharing with him. Ice cream was only the beginning of what she would have enjoyed sharing with him, had the fates been kinder.

One day is all, she reminded herself.

And perhaps, one more kiss, if she couldn't find the strength to resist. But nothing more.

NICK OPENED the car door for Annie and she climbed inside. Sighing, she leaned back on the seat. When Nick drove her home, their day together would end—the only day together they would ever have. It was better that way, and yet . . .

"I hate to see it end."

For a moment, Annie thought she'd spoken her thoughts out loud, only belatedly realizing the words were Nick's.

She gave him a quick smile. "So do I. But you know what they say—all good things must et cetera, et cetera."

He frowned, resting his hands squarely on the steering wheel. "Not necessarily." He started the engine. "How about dinner?"

"I—" Annie clamped her mouth shut. She'd been about to tell him that she wasn't the least bit hungry. Except for his company. She certainly was hungry for that. For a breathless moment she struggled with her conscience. "I'd love to have dinner with you," she said at last.

"Prime rib at the Buena Vista Inn all right?"

A fish taco with chocolate sauce at a greasy spoon would be all right. She said, "That sounds fine."

"Good." His smile dazzled her.

The way he made her feel dazzled her even more.

THEY TALKED, rather than ate, their way through dinner. By mutual consent, they kept the conversation light and non-threatening. To Annie's relief, Robert's name did not arise.

Nick drove her home much later through a moonlit night, the scent of flowers perfuming the air. He pulled into her driveway and turned off the engine. Moving briskly, he climbed out of the car and walked around to open her door.

He offered her a hand and she took it and let him help her out of the car. "Thank you for a lovely time," she said primly, intensely aware that they were still touching.

He stepped closer. With the car behind her, she had no place to retreat . . . had retreat occurred to her. Her throat tightened with tension.

"It doesn't have to be over." He stroked the side of her throat. "The lovely part, anyway."

"Nick . . ." She arched her neck beneath his hand. Then it wasn't his hand at all but his lips, nuzzling aside her hair to press kisses against her throat, beneath the curve of her chin and up to her ear. She felt the flick of his tongue and groaned.

He wrapped one arm around her waist. Exerting pressure at the small of her back, he drew her hard against him. She was beginning to realize that each time he touched her, she responded more quickly. And each time he touched her, she wanted a little more from him—a lot more from him.

He spoke between tiny nibbling kisses. "Ask me to come in." His warm breath sent tendrils of excitement curling through her. "Ask me to come in, Annie."

Before she could respond, his mouth claimed hers. She clung to him, wanting to say yes, knowing she couldn't, terrified she might.

His lips grazed her cheek. "You don't want me to go, Annie. Admit it."

She couldn't lie. "I...I admit it. But I can't ask you in."

He explored the contours of her throat with his mouth, stroking one hand up her side. The backs of his fingers brushed the outer swell of her breast and hesitated. "We're not kids," he murmured, beginning to massage her sensuously. "We can do any damned thing we want to do. Annie, Annie love, this is the right time and place for this sort of thing. Let's go inside."

Her own words! She went rigid in his arms. "But that wasn't what I meant," she cried. "Stop, Nick—please!"

He yanked himself upright and his hands fell away from her. He gave a disgusted grunt, and for a moment stood there breathing hard. At last he spoke, his tone bitter. "I know you were married for years but you still make me feel as if I'm trying to defile a virgin. It's not a feeling I like."

"I'm sorry." Misery washed over her. "I seem to have misled you. It's just...I've already told you I'm not...I'm not capable of having an affair."

"An affair!" he roared. "Who said anything about an affair?"

"What else could you be after?"

Her question hung in the air between them.

With a choked exclamation, he grabbed her elbow and whirled her toward the house, his usually graceful movements jerky and uncoordinated. "I could be after any number of things," he grated.

With nothing more to lose, she spoke without thinking. "Name two! You're my boss, for heaven's sake. You're putting me in an impossible position."

He shot her a black glance. "I think I liked you better as a shrinking violet," he said grimly, halting at the front door.

She pulled her arm free and stepped back, her eyes wide and frightened—not of him but of what he had made her feel. What she still felt. She wanted him. There—she'd admitted it! Him, nobody else.

"Damn it to—" He broke off, glaring at her. "I have no intention of forcing myself on you, so relax." He sucked in a deep breath, calming himself with a visible effort. "Okay, you want it strictly business? Fine. What have you got lined up for the next couple of weeks for your column? Besides the dedication of the new recreation center, of course."

Annie, in the process of inserting the key in the lock, froze. The hair on her head literally stood on end; every nerve in her body tensed. Slowly she faced him.

"The new recreation center?" she repeated, praying she'd heard wrong.

"That's right."

In the amber glow of the porch light, she saw his face harden. The dark shadows beneath his brows and prominent cheekbones gave a demonic cast to his features.

"That's not going to be a problem, is it?" he asked, dangerously calm.

Miserably she looked down at her hands, twisting the key between them. "I can't go to the dedication. You know that. I said I'd never set foot inside that building."

Nick drew back ever so slightly, but ever so significantly. "I thought that was His Honor talking."

Annie forced herself to meet his scornful gaze. "My husband spoke for both of us," she whispered.

Hot anger leaped into his face. "I thought you'd started thinking for yourself," he said with heavy sarcasm. "I see I was wrong." He thrust his hands deep into his trouser pockets, as if to keep from grabbing her and shaking her. "This is a project that will benefit the whole town, but that's not important to you—you'd rather maintain the fiction that Mayor Robert Page never made a mistake, even if it means perpetuating a lie."

"That's not fair," Annie protested. Everything was slipping away—her job, her self-respect...her place in this man's life, however trivial. "I've already compromised on so many of the things Robert stood for. The rec building was his last stand. I have a duty and responsibility to respect his wishes. You just don't understand."

"The hell I don't," Nick flared. His searing glance withered her. "I understand that you don't trust me and that your first loyalty isn't to your job, it's to a memory. I understand just fine. I simply don't agree."

"Th-then..." Annie swallowed hard. "I guess we've reached a stalemate. Perhaps someone else can cover just this one event."

He shook his head decisively. "That's not how it works. Either you do your job or you turn in your Minolta."

"Pentax." She couldn't believe he meant what he was saying. She expected him to relent at any moment.

He didn't. "Whatever," he said coldly. "The dedication's next Saturday. Be there or..."

The words hung in the night air, calm and deadly. "You can't mean that," she whispered.

"I do mean it." The words were clipped and final. "My first impression of you was right. Just because you're beautiful and bright and fun to be around...and I like holding you in my arms and kissing you—"

He looked away for a moment, a muscle jumping in his tight jaw. "I've made a damned fool of myself," he continued softly. "With a little help from you, of course."

She groaned and stepped toward him, lifting her hand in a gesture of supplication. "Oh, Nick, I never intended—"

The door swung open and she let out a startled cry. Nick stepped between her and possible danger, but not before she'd seen who stood there.

Nick cocked his arm for a punch but Annie grabbed him and hung on. "Don't!" she cried. "It's Lew! It's my son!"

Nick swore and dropped his fist. Lew stood in the doorway. His shrewd hazel eyes swung from his stepmother to his father's worst enemy.

"Hi, Mom," he said cheerfully. "Hi, Mr. Kimball. Fancy meeting you here."

CHAPTER NINE

ANNIE THREW HER ARMS around her stepson's neck. "Why didn't you tell me you were coming?" she cried.

"Didn't know myself until the last minute. I hitched a ride with a guy going to San Diego for a family emergency. He had to pass Buena Vista to get there so he dropped me off." Lew's curious gaze went over her shoulder to settle on Nick. "Good to see you again, sir."

"You know each other?" Surprised, Annie glanced from one to the other.

Nick nodded. He was giving Lew the wary courtesy one man gave another when both had an eye on the same territory . . . or the same woman. "You were in high school," Nick said. "Your father introduced us at . . . a high school track meet, I think it was."

Lew grinned. "That's some memory you've got." He extended his hand, his smile open and affable.

The two men shook hands.

Lew nodded toward the interior of the house. "Uh, come on in, Mr. Kimball. I was about to go hit the books when I heard the car, so I won't be in your way."

Annie felt her face flame. Lew couldn't have been any more obvious if he'd tried. "Nick just dropped me off, Lew," she protested hastily. "He's not staying."

"That's right." Nick glanced at his wristwatch with a great show of impatience. "I'll see you next week, Annie." He turned, took two steps and hesitated. Eyeing her over his shoulder, he added with dark certainty, "I meant what I said."

She lifted her chin. "I don't like ultimatums, Nick."

He arched one dark brow. "I don't like people... employees who don't know where their loyalties should lie."

Annie stiffened; Lew's arm tightened around her waist as if in response. They stood on the porch until the tail-lights of Nick's BMW disappeared around a bend.

"Well, well, well," Lew said. "Did the man say employee?"

"I'm afraid so." Annie's head drooped as they turned to go inside. She hadn't missed that speculative note in her stepson's voice. She sighed. "Come into the family room, honey. We have to talk."

Lew sank onto the couch next to her, an expectant expression on his face. Annie had put off this serious discussion for so long that she no longer knew where to begin.

When the silence threatened to become strained, she said, "I thought you'd warn me before you came home, so I'd have time to bring you up-to-date on all that's been going on. I know I should have told you—about my job at the *Bandwagon* and my plans to sell the house and everything. But I didn't want to worry you while your leg was in a cast and you couldn't do anything about it."

Lew lifted his leg and flexed his foot and ankle. "The cast is off. I'm as good as new."

"You sure look it to me." She smiled and patted his hand. "How long will you be here, honey?"

A broad grin split his thin face. He still hadn't filled out to a man's contours but some day he would be as impressive as his father. Impressive, she thought, but never as forbidding. There was a sweetness about Lew that she doubted his father had ever possessed, even in his youth.

"Only a day or two, so talk fast." He settled back on the couch cushions. "Start with Mr. Kimball and this job."

"Mr. Kimball." She licked her lips. "Well, he offered me a job as society columnist at the *Bandwagon*. I decided to take it because we—" she gave him a guilty glance "—I needed the money."

He frowned. "But I thought...." His hazel eyes widened, then narrowed as understanding sank in. "Oh, I get it."

"Don't blame your father, Lew," Annie begged. "He made a few bad investments. He thought there'd be plenty of time to recoup but, well, we never know how much time we've got."

Lew's glance flicked around the nearly bare room. "That explains all these empty spaces. You've even sold off Grandma's rolltop desk."

"I should have told you."

"Damned right, you should have!" He turned an angry face toward her. "I would have helped."

She knew what that meant—exactly what she was determined to prevent. "You're not going to drop out of school and that's final," she told him, her voice rising. "I won't allow it."

He shook his head impatiently, sandy hair falling over his forehead. "We'll talk about me later, Mom. Right now I want to hear about you and Mr. Kimball."

She opened her mouth to reply, realized she didn't know what to say and shut it again. When he refused to fill the awkward gap, she tried again. "I've been lonely," she admitted. "Nick can be a very charming man when he sets his mind to it. Today was ... it wasn't anything important. It just sort of happened."

Lew caught her hands and stared into her eyes, his own probing. She wanted to run away, wanted to conceal her true feelings . . . whatever they might be.

"You like him," Lew announced with youthful certainty. "Maybe even more than like him."

Annie groaned, making a face to cover her embarrassment. "Not at all. He's just—" She shrugged helplessly.

Lew laughed. "Don't try to kid me, Mom. This is great! Does he feel . . . ?" He made a slight rocking motion with one hand, his expression hopeful.

"I don't know *how* he feels and now I never will," she said. "He's been very nice to me, mostly, right up until tonight."

"Did he propose? Is that why the two of you looked so guilty?"

"No!" She stared at him, shocked to the core.

"Then what?" he pressed. Suddenly his young face hardened. "Did he ask you to live with him?"

Annie sprang to her feet. "You can't talk this way to your mother, Lewis Puller Page! If you were a little younger, I'd wash your mouth out with soap."

"Then how'd he get you so upset?"

"He asked me to cover the dedication of the new recreation center for my column, that's how." She clenched her hands into fists and glared at her stepson, transferring all her fury to him. "Asked me? He told me! And I told him—"

"That you'll do it, I hope."

"Of course not." She whirled away and began to pace. "You know I can't. It would break your father's heart if I went back on his word."

"Jeez, Mom! Wake up!" Lew bolted upright. "My father is dead!" He yelled the words, a wealth of anger and pain behind them. "You're not married anymore, not to him or anybody."

He'd never spoken to her that way, not ever. Her lower lip trembled and she clamped it between her teeth for a moment until she regained control. "Don't you think I know that?" she demanded in a low, intense voice.

"Then quit living like you expect him to show up any day and hold an inspection, okay?" Lew's cheeks were flushed and his eyes held a suspicious glitter. "You've got to make your own judgments now, not try and second-guess what Dad would have wanted."

She sat back down beside him. "I didn't realize how angry you still are at your father," she said softly. "I'm sorry."

She saw him through a haze of tears, which she tried to swallow back. Wordlessly she reached for him, and he came into her arms like the little boy he once was. For a moment she held him, his head a welcome weight against her shoulder.

She felt him draw a shuddering breath, and then he sat up, brushing awkwardly at his eyes.

"I'm not mad at him, Mom," Lew said in a voice that cracked. "It took a while but I think there at the end, he even admired me for standing up to him." He gave her a crooked little smile. "Dad wasn't perfect but neither was ... neither am I."

"Lew—"

"No, Mom, listen." He caught her hands in his and stared earnestly into her eyes. "I don't care about this house, or any money he did or didn't leave us. I'm twenty-one years old—we can get by."

She had never been prouder of her son than at that moment. "Once I sell this house, there'll be plenty of money, at least for essentials," she said. "And there's nothing more essential than your education."

His jaw jutted out. "What about you? If you think—"

"I'll be fine. I'll be able to live much more simply, and I do have my..." Her voice trailed off; she'd been about to say she had her job, but as of next Saturday, that would no longer be true.

He watched her closely. "Have your what?"

She sighed. "My pride," she improvised. "Lew, I won't betray your father by going to that opening. All my life I've believed in certain principles of duty and honor and loyalty. I can't turn my back on that now."

"That's pride talking all right, but I guess without it, you wouldn't be you." He leaned forward and kissed her cheek. "I love you, Mom," he said, his voice gruff. He cleared his throat and jumped to his feet. "Personally, I hope you'll reconsider, but I'm with you all the way, no matter what."

Loyalty, apparently, ran in the family.

LEW'S RIDE RETURNED the following afternoon and the two young men prepared to head back north.

"I'll be gainfully employed by the end of this week," Lew promised, pausing in the doorway. "I'll be back home in about three weeks and we'll sit down and figure everything out."

"It's nothing you have to worry about," Annie insisted. "I'll handle it."

She saw the disappointment on his face. "Mom, I'm not a kid anymore," he said. "Let me act like a man, for once."

She recoiled from the steel edge to his voice, only later recognizing the truth in his words. She did treat him like a kid; she always had, perhaps because his father had treated him like a Marine private.

When Lew had gone, she called her real estate agent. "List the house. The sooner I can get out from under this place the better," she told him, surprised and pleased by her own candor.

Wednesday she stopped by the *Bandwagon* to drop off film. She could barely control her nerves. She craved the sight of Nick, but at the same time she dreaded seeing him because of the way they'd parted.

Roz walked out of the darkroom with Pete as Annie raised her hand to knock on the door. The editor did not smile. "Got time for a cup of coffee?" she asked.

"Sure." Annie handed the camera to the photographer. "Can I get the camera loaded first?"

"No." Roz turned to Pete. "Load it and leave it on my desk. She can pick it up there."

Unhappy with this turn of events, Annie followed Roz upstairs to the lunchroom. At midafternoon, they had the place to themselves. Roz pulled two mugs from a rack behind the coffeepot and poured.

She offered a mug to Annie. "Cheers," she said bleakly.

Annie was so nervous she didn't even add sugar to her cup. "Is something wrong?" she asked. "I have the distinct feeling I'm in trouble. If you're concerned about that fashion show in Sunday's column—"

"No, no, that's not it." Roz pulled out a chair and sat down, placing her mug on the table. "I know Nick spoke to you about that." She gave an exasperated sigh. "I don't mean to stick my nose into your business but you look just as miserable as he does."

He? Nick, miserable? Annie gulped and sat down at the table across from Roz. Why should Nick be miserable? "I don't exactly know what you're talking about," she admitted.

"Yes, you do." Roz sounded angry. "I'm talking about Nick and you darn well know it. He tells me chances are slim to none that you'll cover the dedication of the new community center next Saturday. And if you don't—" She drew one forefinger across her throat with appropriate sound effects.

"That's right." Annie's voice sounded as stiff and cold as she felt. "And I won't."

Roz leaned forward, her forearms on the table. "Don't do this, Annie," she said fervently. "You and Nick are wonderful together. You can't imagine what a good influence you were on him. But now he's reverted to his old, cynical self." She rolled her eyes. "Reverted? He's worse than he ever was. The man's a bear. Unless the two of you work this out, I don't know what's going to happen to those of us unfortunate enough to be caught in the cross fire."

Annie didn't believe for a minute that she'd had any kind of positive effect on the strong-willed Nicholas Kimball. "You must be mistaken," she said. "The only effect I've had on him has been a bad one. You're way off base, Roz."

"My Lord but you're blind!" Roz slapped one hand on the tabletop so hard the contents of her cup sloshed over. "Do us all a favor and cover that grand opening. If you don't, you'll regret it for the rest of your life." She rolled her eyes. "And so will every employee of the Buena Vista *Bandwagon*."

Annie shook her head. "I can't. I want to but I can't."

"Because of Robert?" Roz pursed her lips. "Nobody's going to hold you to something your late husband said in

Without taking his eyes off Annie's face, Nick spoke to Roz. "Leave us alone for a minute. There's something I want to say to Annie."

"Sure thing, boss."

Annie stood perfectly still while Roz hurried past and disappeared down the stairs. It took all her resolve to pretend to be unmoved by his nearness, and she thought he must surely see how agitated she was beneath the surface.

When they were alone, he let out his breath in a gust of sound. With a distracted movement, he shoved one hand through his hair, mussing it up in the process.

"Annie, I—" He bit off his words.

"Yes?" She could barely force the word past stiff lips. Her face felt as if it would never smile again.

"Damnation," he muttered. He shook his head, his expression pained. "I'm either coming down with something or falling in love with you. Whichever it is, I guess I can get over it. What the hell—in for a penny, in for a pound."

He swept her into his arms before she could muster a protest, swooping her over backward. Her hands flew to his shoulders and she hung on—in the interests of self-preservation, of course.

He peered down into her startled face. "Yeah," he grated. "But I'm no patsy. I *will* get over it." He groaned. "Maybe."

He kissed her.

The fierce tenderness of his mouth overwhelmed her. With a choked cry, she slid her arms around his neck. Her lips parted, welcoming the thrust of his tongue with an urgency born of desperation.

She had never known what it meant, to want a man so much she ached with it. Her body burned where it touched his, but the wildest flame raged inside, bringing her blood to a boil and turning her to cinders.

He lifted his head and whispered her name in a voice that betrayed a yearning equal to her own. She pressed her forehead to his lips and closed her eyes.

"Don't say anything," she begged. "If you do you'll ruin it."

"I have to. Say something, I mean, not ruin anything."

He straightened and pulled her upright, his hands shaking. He slid his arms over hers in a loose embrace. She slipped her own arms around his waist beneath his jacket, her hands clutching at his lean sides.

"Look," he said forcefully, "I'm not just out for a cheap affair, regardless of what you thought. We've got something special going here. All we have to do is get past this one last thing—not a big thing, really. If you'll just come to the damned dedication—"

She shoved herself out of his embrace. "You never give up, do you?" She felt the blood rush into her face and didn't care. Anger seemed the most appropriate response. Certainly the safest. "If it's not a big thing, why don't *you* concede the point?"

"Because there's a principle involved!" he roared. "I'm running a newspaper, not a finishing school. You think reporters get to pick and choose their assignments? Hell, no!"

For a moment they stood there, anger holding them motionless. Annie felt the pressure rise inside her until it seemed she'd burst like an overfilled balloon. When the tension became unbearable, she passed over an invisible dividing line and into some kind of numb purgatory. Rational thought became possible once more.

"This isn't a matter of journalistic ethics," she said. Her voice, although shaky, was surprisingly controlled.

"No?" he challenged. "What is it, then?"

"Your final victory over an old enemy. This is the last bone of contention. I've given on every other point. I—"

"The hell you have! You've been running me around in circles."

She shook her head slowly. "You see things your way and I see them mine. It's obvious we'll never see eye to eye, so it's better not to try."

There, that wasn't so hard, she told herself. She walked around him toward the stairway, ever so calmly. All she had to do was hold it together until she got out of there.

"Annie?"

She heard the strain in his voice and stopped, keeping her back very straight. "Yes?"

"There's one thing wrong with what you just said."

"Oh? And what might that be?"

"You love me."

Her heart leaped and settled into a wild pounding. For a moment she couldn't answer, and then she said, almost gently, "If I do, I'll get over it."

Roz PEERED into the lunchroom and looked around cautiously. Nick, sitting at a table with his head resting on his hands, saw her and glared. The last thing he needed was company.

"You alone?" she asked, clearly disappointed.

"Do you see anyone else here?" he demanded, using sarcasm as a defense.

"No, but I didn't see Annie leave, either," Roz said tartly. "She didn't stop by to pick up her camera."

"It's not her camera, it's the paper's."

"Whatever."

She walked to the end of the table and leaned against it. "I take it things didn't go well."

Nick's lip curled in an approximation of a smile. "If it had, she'd have picked up the camera," he pointed out. "She's gone. Do you think Nadine would come back?"

Roz's eyes flashed. "Over my dead body!" She leaned forward, her stance aggressive. "So what'll you do next?"

"About what?"

"Getting Annie to change her mind."

Nick reared back. "Nothing. Not a damned thing."

She stared at him. "I can't believe you're giving up on her so easily with so much at stake."

"At stake!" He howled the words. "There's nothing at stake except a damned newspaper column and we'll find someone to handle that if I have to do it myself."

He surged to his feet and they faced each other across the table. Nick, shoulders tense, gave his editor his most ferocious scowl. To his displeasure, she returned it—with interest.

"Don't burn your bridges," she advised.

"I didn't! She did!" Nick's voice reverberated through the room and he turned down the volume a notch. "She won't be there Saturday."

"Who can blame her, if you asked her this nicely!" Roz turned and stomped toward the stairs.

Alarmed, Nick called after her. "Hey, you're not walking out on me too, are you?"

She half turned, her hands planted on her hips. "No. Would you care if I did?"

"Certainly," he said, feeling both injured and picked on. It seemed as if all the women in his life were ganging up on him. "What do you women want from a man, blood?"

Rosalind arched her left eyebrow and gave him a cool once-over. "If you think about that question, you may be able to figure out the answer all by yourself. I hope to heaven it comes to you by Saturday."

"Now wait a minute, Roz." He followed her down the stairs, talking to the back of her head. He didn't care whether she answered him or not. All he wanted was a distraction from dismal thoughts of Annie Page.

Who, apparently, was still in love with her dead husband.

CHAPTER TEN

ANNIE AND THE OTHER eleven members of the Buena Vista Cultural Foundation board spent Friday morning touring sites proposed for a new community auditorium. By mutual consent, they then repaired to Hoffy's Coffee Shop to talk over their findings.

One by one board members departed until only Annie and Larry Rayburn remained. She gave him a tentative smile, which he returned somewhat absently. *It's fate,* she decided. *I'll ask him flat out for a job.*

This time, nothing would stop her—not pride, not embarrassment, not anything.

Larry glanced at his watch. "I've got to be moving along, too," he announced. "Can I drop you somewhere or do you have your car?"

"I have my car but—" She took a deep breath. "There's something I'd like to talk to you about before you go, Larry."

"Sure." He settled back in the orange plastic booth and eyed her expectantly.

Just as she opened her mouth to say "I'm looking for a job and I'm not kidding," he looked past her.

"Hey, your boss just came in," he said with enthusiasm. "Maybe he'll join us." He waved.

"Larry, *don't*!" Annie twisted around. Across the room, she saw Nick glance her way. He did not smile, nor did she. He lifted one hand in a dismissive salute and turned his head to speak to the woman at his side.

Annie caught her breath. The woman was young and blond and *gorgeous*. Flouncing around on her seat, Annie's dismayed glance met Larry's confused one.

"What's wrong with him?" Larry wondered. "Not very friendly, I'd say." He brightened. "But that's some dish with him—hubba hubba!"

"Hubba hubba?" In spite of her chagrin, Annie laughed. "You must be older than you look, Larry." He gave her a rueful smile, and she added, "But he's not my boss. Not anymore."

Out of the corner of her eye, she saw Connie approach Nick and the blond woman, who were waiting to be seated. Annie dragged her attention back to Larry, who looked astonished by her piece of news. As indeed had everyone who'd heard it thus far.

"What happened?" he asked. "I was just getting used to the idea."

She shrugged. "A little difference of opinion."

"And he fired you?"

"Certainly not! I quit."

Connie led Nick and his companion toward a booth in the opposite corner of the room—the corner where Annie's eyes fell each time she looked up. She forced herself to concentrate on her companion.

"Well," Larry said, "maybe it's for the best. It's not as if you need the money, so why take the grief?"

"But I do need the money." She spoke in a low voice. "I'm looking for another job. That's what I wanted to talk to you about."

His mouth fell open. "Then you mean, when you came into my store a few weeks ago you were serious?"

She nodded humbly. "I was a little embarrassed about it then, but the time for false pride is past. I'm selling my house and moving to a smaller place and looking for a job. I wonder...do you have any openings at your store?"

He looked genuinely regretful. "Gosh, Annie, I wish I'd known. I just hired a salesclerk last week."

"Oh." Deflated, she stared at her empty coffee cup. Well, she thought, at least she'd asked; that was a victory in itself. "Maybe you'll keep me in mind if anything else comes up," she suggested.

"Why, sure. I—"

Connie stopped beside the booth and he broke off. The waitress was popping gum and grinning.

"The ball and chain's on the phone for you, Larry," she said cheerfully. "You can take it back behind the cash register." She winked at Annie and walked away.

"Be right back." Larry slid out of the booth.

Almost as if on cue, Nick rose from his seat across the room and walked straight toward Annie. She braced herself. She should simply stand up and leave before he reached her, she told herself. But she had missed him so much, and he looked so wonderful, even with that grim expression on his face. *I must be strong,* she told herself, as her resolve weakened.

He stopped beside the booth and looked down at her. A muscle twitched in his rigid jaw, but that was all. He had looked at her just that way during her marriage, as if she were an unknown quality in which he had no real interest.

"How's it going?" he demanded, his manner brusque.

"Don't ask," she said, not smiling.

"You could always change your mind."

"So could you."

His eyes narrowed. "I was a damned fool to get my hopes up. Lord, you're stubborn."

"Not stubborn," Annie corrected, relying on anger to keep her voice strong. "Consistent." She picked up her coffee cup with hands that trembled; she put the cup quickly back on the saucer. "I will never set foot inside that recreation center. End of conversation."

"'Consistency is the hobgoblin of little minds.'" Nick leaned over the table, placing his palms flat on its surface. Blue fire leaped in the depths of his eyes. "Besides, this isn't about the recreation center anymore. Deny it all you want but it's still about you and me."

It was as if he spoke into a vacuum; his words rang through the suddenly quiet coffee shop. Annie recoiled, her alarmed gaze flying around the room. Everyone was staring.

She felt embarrassed color flame in her cheeks. "When you walked in here with that . . . that *woman*, I naturally assumed there was no 'you and me.'"

"Huh?" He frowned and glanced over his shoulder toward the blonde waiting in his booth. "Her? She's no woman, she's a flack."

Now it was Annie's turn to be confused. "A flack?"

"A PR person. You know, public relations? She's trying to talk me into running a story we both know is puff because her company's too cheap to buy an ad." He stared at Annie for a moment, his eyes widening. "You're jealous!"

"Be quiet!" She peered around guiltily. They might as well be the floor show, with all the interest they were generating. Belatedly she added, "I am not jealous. And please don't shout—you're attracting attention."

"What do I care?" He straightened and shoved his hands deep into the pockets of his trousers, never taking his gaze from her face. He did, however, lower his voice. "This isn't about the rec center and it isn't about that blonde. It's about you and me...and Robert. Do you have any idea how hard it is to fight a ghost?"

"Then don't," she said. "Don't!" She stood up unsteadily, feeling trapped. "That's all this is to you, another fight. One final chance to beat Robert, and you've got to take it."

"What are you talking about?" He frowned. "I don't give a—" He ground his teeth. "Robert's dead and I'm alive. I didn't plan it that way—it's the luck of the draw. Are you going to devote the rest of your life to his memory? If you are, include me out."

"I never included you in!" Her voice rose, despite her intentions to the contrary. Clenching her hands into fists, she leaned forward toward him, speaking furiously. "*You* came to *me*, remember? *You* conned *me* into taking that cockamamy job for which I was totally unprepared. *You* made passes at *me*, and then when I started to...started to..."

She floundered, breathing hard. She sank down onto the booth. Tears crowded at the backs of her eyelids and she knew she was about to break down.

"Started to what?" he challenged, his low voice intense. "Fall in love with me?"

"When I started to...to not hate you, only then did you inform me that it's all or nothing. Well, I choose nothing!"

"You don't mean that."

"I do!" She was practically screaming, audience be damned. "There's no way I'm going to humiliate Robert by setting foot in that blasted building, tomorrow or ever! That would be...treason!"

She pushed herself to her feet and he didn't try to stop her. Head high, she walked what seemed like miles across the room to the door. Larry stood near the cash register, gaping.

Annie paused beside him. "Is everything all right?" she asked in a strangled voice.

"Wh-what?" Larry stammered.

She nodded at the telephone on the counter. "Your wife."

No response.

"On the telephone?"

Larry started. "Oh, that. I guess Connie made a mistake. There was nobody on the line."

Annie's lips tightened. She didn't believe for a minute that Connie had made a mistake.

THE SONG OF BIRDS awakened Annie Saturday morning. Moaning piteously, she pulled her pillow over her head and squeezed her eyes closed.

In all the world, she wanted nothing more than for this day to be done and gone. She didn't want to go anywhere or do anything or see anyone—maybe ever. Certainly not until after the dedication ceremony.

Dragging herself out of bed, she crossed to the window and peered out. She saw one of those wretched Southern California days, picture perfect with brilliant sunshine and not so much as a hint of smog.

It made her sick just to look at it.

She was outside in that sunshine, trimming the hedges in front of the house, when the telephone rang for the first time that day. She felt a tremor of apprehension and deliberately let the answering machine handle the call. If it was Lew, she'd call him later. If it was Nick...*Please, Lord, let it be Nick*.

It was, in fact, neither. When she played the message, she heard the sprightly voice of Edna Peck. "Annie, I hate to bother you but I'm worried about Henrietta. We're all going off to that dedication ceremony this afternoon and I just know she's going to be left at the Senior Center all alone. She keeps telling me that son of hers will be picking her up and taking her over there, but I'm not so sure. If you happen to drop by the Center, be sure and check on her. She likes you. Thanks.''

Annie frowned at the offending telephone. This really put her on the spot, she realized unhappily. Henrietta Kopeckne was one of Annie's favorites, for reasons that totally escaped her. Why she felt so drawn to the crusty old woman, Annie couldn't imagine.

She glanced at her wristwatch. It was a few minutes past one and the dedication was scheduled for two o'clock. She didn't have a lot of time to make up her mind, if she intended to drop Henrietta off for the festivities.

She didn't need a lot of time, she admitted as she took off her jeans and sweatshirt and stared into her closet. She couldn't turn her back on someone who might need her. Automatically she reached for a conservative white pleated skirt and navy blouse. A flash of aqua caught her eye and she hesitated.

She hadn't worn that particular dress in years and wasn't even sure why it still hung in her closet. Slowly she pulled it out and examined it.

The bodice was white, the flared skirt aqua with a pattern of tiny white dots. A wide midriff band set off a narrow matching belt, making the waist look indecently small.

She sighed. Robert had never liked the dress, although he hadn't volunteered that information. She'd worn it a couple of summers before innocently remarking that it was one of her favorites.

He'd looked unimpressed.

"Don't you think it's pretty?" she's pressed, thinking somewhat foolishly that she'd draw a rare compliment from him. It was one of the most flattering garments she owned.

"Not much," he'd said. "It's a bit frivolous."

Crushed, she'd not worn the dress since. Looking at it, she wondered why. "Frivolous" wasn't the worst thing a dress could be called.

It occurred to her now that it hadn't been what Robert said at all. She'd turned against the dress because he hadn't cared enough to even tell her he disliked it, until she forced the issue.

ANNIE WALKED into the game room of the Buena Vista Senior Citizens' Center and there sat Henrietta Kopeckne in her wheelchair. She wore a navy dress, and around her neck she'd wrapped a long string of the most beautiful pearls Annie had ever seen.

"Good afternoon, Mrs. Kopeckne," Annie greeted. "You look great. Going somewhere?"

Mrs. Kopeckne looked surprised and flustered. "Yes, dear. My son is picking me up to take me to the dedication of the new building. He'll be here any minute." She twisted gnarled hands together in her lap as she spoke.

"In that case, why don't I keep you company until he arrives? I'm a little at loose ends today myself."

Mrs. Kopeckne's lower lip trembled. "You don't need to do that," she protested. "You run along and—" The telephone in the lobby rang and Mrs. Kopeckne started and glanced wildly toward the sound.

Annie patted the old lady's arm. "I'll get that and be right back," she promised.

For a moment, Mrs. Kopeckne looked as if she might argue. Instead, she slumped in her wheelchair with the barest of nods. Her reaction struck Annie as odd, but she shrugged it off as she went to answer the phone.

"Buena Vista Senior Center. This is Annie Page—may I help you?"

"I hope so. This is Mr. William Kopeckne's secretary." The voice was cool and professional. "Is Mr. Kopeckne's mother still there?"

"Why, yes. Would you like me to bring her to the phone?"

"No need." The secretary sighed. "Mr. Kopeckne won't be pleased—he thought she was going to the ceremony with her friends and that they'd drop her off at home later. Just on the outside chance she didn't, he asked me to call and tell her that Billy won't be able to pick her up until five this afternoon."

Oh, that poor, poor woman. "She'll be so disappointed. She's waiting right now for her son."

"You must be mistaken." The secretary sounded exasperated. "She's known all along that there was only an outside chance Mr. Kopeckne would be able to take the time to humor her on this matter."

She doesn't mean "take the time," Annie thought. *She means "waste the time."* Her hand clenched on the receiver. "I don't want to be disagreeable but the woman is waiting for her son to pick her up. She couldn't have understood."

"Believe me, she did." The secretary's voice sharpened. "I explained the situation to her myself, hours ago. Please—just tell her Billy will be there at five. Thank you so much."

The line went dead. Annie hung up the receiver and stood there, feeling sick. What should she say to Mrs. Kopeckne?

Her son had disappointed her again; her son *always* disappointed her. Edna knew it, Annie finally knew it, and even Henrietta must accept it by now. False pride had kept her there despite the efforts of those who loved her—the friends who had tried to get her to accompany them to the festivities. False pride made her deny the truth—that her son had his own best interests at heart, not hers.

Just as false pride kept Annie there, over the protestations of one who loved her. As false pride had made her deny the truth—that Robert, too, had had his own best interests at heart.

Slowly she walked back into the game room and looked at the proud old lady. For one flashing instant, Annie didn't see Mrs. Kopeckne; she saw her own figure—an old woman isolated by an inflexible pride that robbed her of every chance of happiness.

But it wasn't too late—it couldn't be, not for either of them. Annie's heart swelled with gratitude for the lesson she'd just learned.

Robert hadn't been infallible. He'd been a good man capable of making mistakes, just like everyone else. She'd been a true and loyal wife to him but now he was dead. She would always honor his memory but it was time to tear down the shrine she'd erected in her heart.

Robert had been wrong about the recreation center and wrong about Nick.

"Oh, Mrs. Kopeckne!" Annie knelt and threw her arms around the startled woman's neck, giving her a big hug. "Please go to the ceremony with me!"

"Good heavens, girl!" Mrs. Kopeckne tried to brush Annie away. "I can't do that—what would my son think? What would my friends think? No, no, it's out of the question."

"Please?" Annie could hardly believe what she intended to do. *But I know stubborn pride when I see it,* she thought. *I should. I've had enough experience with it.* "It looks like your son's been delayed. He wouldn't want you to miss the fun."

"I...I..." Mrs. Kopeckne swallowed hard and her faded eyes brimmed with tears. "I don't want anyone to know," she whispered.

"Know what?" Annie pressed gently. It somehow seemed important for Mrs. Kopeckne to face the truth. As Annie had faced it.

"He promised he'd come, and then *that woman* called and said...but if I go without him, it would look bad, don't you see?" She turned a beseeching face to Annie. "I do have my pride," she added with forlorn dignity.

So do I, and look where it got me, Annie thought, her heart breaking. She caught the trembling blue-veined hands in hers. *If I end up like Mrs. Kopeckne, it won't be because I didn't try,* she vowed.

She loved Nicholas Kimball and she'd do anything she had to do to convince him that he'd never have to compete with a ghost again. What she'd felt for Robert was a match flame, compared to the raging conflagration Nick ignited inside her.

She gave the elderly woman's hand a final comforting squeeze and stood up. "Mrs. Kopeckne," she said, her voice trembling but sure, "we're cutting off our noses to spite our faces, the both of us. I'm going to that ceremony and so are you, if I have to kidnap you!"

She added a silent prayer that she wouldn't be too late.

NICK STOOD IN THE WINGS behind the stage of the new recreation center, peering out at the noisy crowd. Metal chairs in precise rows marched the length of the polished wooden floor, all of them filled. Late arrivals stood in the back of the room, four and five deep in some places.

The person he most wanted to see was not among those assembled.

I wish Annie were here to see this, he thought with genuine longing and not a trace of smugness. *She'd realize how welcome this community project really is.*

She'd realize that I was right and she was wrong.

Nick stifled a groan and turned away, unconsciously crumpling the sheaf of papers he held in his hand. Who was right and who was wrong no longer mattered. Either she loved him or she didn't. If she loved him, she'd be there.

If he loved her, would he insist on that?

Mitch Priddy approached. "Almost time to start," he announced. "I appreciate your participation, Nick, under the circumstances."

"What circumstances?" Nick barked the question, glaring at the shorter man.

Mitch seemed unfazed. "That business with Annie Page. Everyone in town knows about the blow-up in Hoffy's."

"What!"

"Sure. Most people think you fired her but I think she quit. Anyway, if you're at your most charming today, you should be able to win over a few of the doubters."

"Priddy, some day you'll go too far."

Something in Nick's deadly-dark tone must have got through to the usually unflappable city manager because he blanched and took a step back. "Oops. This is apparently that day. Why don't I just run along while I'm still able to."

Simmering, Nick leaned against the wall and watched while the chairman of the Parks and Recreation Commission got the ceremonies under way. All the pleasure he had anticipated upon this occasion seemed tainted. What should have felt like a victory tasted like a defeat.

The amplified voice droned on in the background. "I'm pleased at this time to introduce the man perhaps more instrumental than any other in making this community project a reality."

Nick jerked his skittering attention back to the business at hand. Seemed they were laying it on a bit thick, he thought morosely. *If it wasn't for this damned building, Annie and I—*

"—Mr. Nick Kimball, publisher of the Buena Vista *Bandwagon* and one of the earliest, and I might add loudest, proponents of the Buena Vista Recreation Center."

Nick strode onto the stage to applause he interpreted as merely polite. *Fine,* he thought. *It's not a newspaper's job to be loved by the masses. It's a newspaper's job to print the news and raise hell.*

Stepping to the mike, he spread the wrinkled pages of his speech on the podium and glowered at the audience. He knew most of the people gathered here and they knew him, at least superficially. The city's finest—the movers, the shakers, the workers.

He'd have traded the whole damned bunch for one small brunette with the pride of a lion. He'd track her down as soon as he could get out of there, and force her to admit she loved him and couldn't live without him.

His mind made up, he began to speak, his impatience only partially contained. "Fellow Buena Vistans, it's an honor and a privilege for me to be with you here today."

A slight commotion erupted in the back of the auditorium, and he glanced up, irritated at the interruption. *Just let me get through this and out of here,* he thought fervently. He caught sight of a wheelchair moving through the standing-room-only crowd and his mood lightened a bit. Mrs. Kopeckne was a dour old lady but he liked her anyway.

He lifted his gaze, expecting to see her grandson Billy pushing the wheelchair, and looked full into the face of Annie Page. Nick's breath whooshed out so forcefully that it sounded like a gale-force wind when amplified by the microphone. Total silence descended on the huge room.

Even from where he stood, he could see the blush rise in her cheeks. She lifted her head proudly. She had never looked more beautiful to him than at that moment, bravely facing the kind of public scrutiny she hated as heads turned toward her.

Nick's eyes met hers. Deliberately she lifted one hand to her lips . . . and blew him a kiss.

A kiss!

Nick felt a silly smile spread over his face. She loved him. No other power on earth could have brought her here today. No other power on earth could have caused her to swallow her pride and deliberately contribute to public speculation.

She loves me!

He looked down helplessly at the pages of his speech, then back at the crowd. People were beginning to stir. Some giggled and cast furtive glances between the front and the back of the room, while others seemed confused by the break in the proceedings.

There was no way now that Nick could get through what was essentially a boring speech. He picked up the sheets of paper, gave Annie a crooked smile and tossed the script into the air.

"To hell with it," he announced into the mike as paper floated to the floor. "I declare this facility open, and may it bring to the citizens of our fair city the same pleasure and happiness it's just brought me."

In the shocked silence, he jumped off the stage. He had a quick impression of Roz, in the front row with her husband. She smiled and flashed a quick thumbs-up.

Then Nick only had eyes for Annie. Long strides carried him down the center aisle. In the general buzz of excitement, he heard a stage whisper: "Hey, isn't that the mayor's wife back there? I thought she was never going to set foot in this place."

And the answer: "Not the mayor's wife, you dodo, his widow. And he was the one all worked up about this place, not her. Annie's got more sense."

Annie welcomed Nick with a nervous smile but kept the wheelchair between them. "Hi," she said breathlessly. "I thought—"

"Thoughts be damned!" He leaned over Mrs. Kopeckne, grasped the handles of her chair and swung it to one side. Before Annie could protest, he swept her into his arms.

She hid her flaming face in his chest. "Nick, you're embarrassing me," she choked, but her fingers dug into his lapels to hold him closer.

"Oh, Annie, Annie." He buried his face in her sweet-smelling hair. "I didn't think you'd show up. I was coming to get you as soon as this was over."

"Were you?" She lifted her radiant face. "Looks like I saved you a trip." She stood on tiptoe to whisper in his ear: "I love you, Nicholas Kimball."

Laughter bubbled in his throat, laughter more joyous than any he'd ever known. He loved this woman, and the minute he saw her walk into the room, he'd known she returned that love.

But he wanted to make it official. "I love you, too," he said fiercely. He wanted to shout it; he wanted to drag her back to the microphone and tell the world. He wanted it on the front page of the *Bandwagon* and the lead story on the six o'clock news.

"Kiss her!" somebody yelled from the audience, and others picked up the cry. "Kiss her! Kiss her!"

Annie's smile was tremulous as she struggled to ignore the escalating bedlam. With all the sound rocketing around them, he read her words on her lips more than heard them: "Is this where I say I've been a fool?"

He shook his head decisively. "This is where I say we're going to have to find a new name for the Society Page. The Society Kimball sounds downright stupid."

And at last he gave in to his own inclination and the exhortations of the crowd.

EPILOGUE

Editor's Note: Our regular society columnist, Annie Page Kimball, is on her honeymoon. In her absence, former Bandwagon columnist Nadine Reed is graciously filling in. Here is Nadine's special report.

ANNIE GROANED luxuriously and rolled over in the enormous bed, sliding a bit on the ivory satin sheet. Her new husband leaned down and gave her a lingering kiss, which quickly threatened to flame out of control.

Nick pulled back just in time. "Wait a minute, wait a minute. You've got to hear this first," he insisted, sinking onto the edge of the bed and shaking out the newspaper he'd just removed from a manila envelope. "Roz went to a lot of trouble to express this all the way to Acapulco for our pleasure and edification."

"Umm..." Annie curled her body around his and kissed his bare thigh. She felt his muscles contract and smiled. "Pleasure and edification," she murmured. "Lord, Nick, how much can one woman take?"

He gave her a smile rich with promise. "We'll certainly find out . . . very soon. Aren't you at least a little curious? The headline is 'A Match Made in Heaven.'" He began to read:

Surprise was the order of the day when Mr. and Mrs. Nicholas Kimball slipped back into town following

*their brief flight from humdrum reality to tie the
martial knot—*

"I'm sorry?" Annie interrupted, caught up in the
flow—or lack of flow—of Nadine's purple prose. "Do you
mean *marital* knot?"

Nick winked. "The jury's still out on that," he said.
"This is Nadine's version. To continue—"

*—to tie the martial knot on Thanksgiving Day in our
sister state of Las Vegas with officiating by a judge
friend of the comely and debonair groom's. Of
course, everyone knows his fairly winsome bride as
the former Annie Page, widow of our lately beloved
mayor Robert and best friend of the groom.*

"But-but—!"

"Let it alone, Annie." He touched loving fingers to her
sputtering lips. "By this time next week, most everyone
will accept it as fact, that Robert and I were boon com-
panions. The feud will be forgotten. As it should be."

She sighed and kissed his fingers. Wrapping her arms
around his waist, she nestled her head on his lap. Let bygones be bygones, she thought, her heart swelling with
happiness.

*Friends of the fortuitous couple espoused tradition by
planning the surprise and gala reception at the popular new Buena Vista Recreation Center. The bride was
all aglow as she was twirled around the dance floor by
her beloved while Sammy and his Swinging Seniors
asked the musical question, "I love you truly."*

*The groom is the highly esteemed publisher of this
newspaper and boss of this reporter. The new "Mrs.
Boss" is Buena Vista's beloved "Citizen of the Year."*

Annie ground her teeth. "This woman is mad," she declared, indignation lifting her head from its delightful resting place. "Mrs. Boss—next thing you know she'll be telling the whole world where we've gone on our secret honeymoon. She's a menace!"

Nick slid one hand down her bare back and she caught her breath, arching against him. "So I've been told." His voice was a velvet purr. "Let me read the rest while I still can."

To which this reporter responds, "Ain't love grand?"

"Ohh, Nick..." Annie closed her eyes against the wealth of sensations aroused by his stroking fingertips. They'd been married for only five days but they'd been the happiest five days of her entire life. Alone together...their whereabouts a secret...no telephone calls, no obligations to anything or anyone other than each other. Paradise.

Nick's muscles trembled; he cleared his throat. "Look, Annie," he said in a raspy voice, "let me finish reading this, okay?"

She raised her head to nip delicately at his corded abdomen. "By all means," she murmured. "Don't mind me."

"There's just one more paragraph." He drew a raggedly determined breath and read:

Enjoy your honeymoon in Acapulco, kids. You deserve nothing but the best! Hey, folks, let's show Nick and Annie how much we miss them. Call them with your best greetings and felicitations at the Hotel Caliente de...

H A R L E Q U I N

Romance®

Coming Next Month

#3103 TO TAME A COWBOY Katherine Arthur
Jennifer needed to get away from the city, her parents' bickering and a violent
boyfriend. A ranch in Montana seems far enough, her new boss Clay Cooper a warm
generous man. Jennifer begins to relax until she finds herself an unwilling
participant in another family's row!

#3104 CITY GIRL, COUNTRY GIRL Amanda Clark
Stung by a bee, knocked down by a huge muddy dog—that's Hannah's introduction
to country life. So the last thing she expects is to actually *enjoy* the enforced
vacation. Or to fall in love with a country vet named Jake McCabe....

#3105 THE GIRL WITH GREEN EYES Betty Neels
When Lucy meets eminent pediatrician William Thurloe, she determines to become
the woman of his dreams. The fact she is neither clever nor sophisticated like Fiona
Seymour, who wants William, too, is just one small obstacle she has to overcome.

#3106 OF RASCALS AND RAINBOWS Marcella Thompson
Kristy Cunningham races to Mount Ida, Arkansas, to find her missing grandfather.
She runs up against her granddad's young partner and self-proclaimed protector—
and the strangest feeling that she must stay, no matter what....

#3107 THE GOLDEN THIEF Kate Walker
Leigh Benedict seems to think every young aspiring actress is a pushover for the
casting couch, and his cynical attitude appalls Jassy. But the attraction that flows
between them makes it difficult for her to convince him otherwise.

#3108 THAI SILK Anne Weale
Clary helps a fellow Briton in trouble in Thailand by summoning Alistair Lincoln
halfway around the world to bail out his stepsister. But when he insists on Clary
sharing responsiblity for young Nina, it's Alistair who becomes the problem.

**Available in February wherever paperback books are sold, or through
Harlequin Reader Service:**

In the U.S.
901 Fuhrmann Blvd.
P.O. Box 1397
Buffalo, N.Y. 14240-1397

In Canada
P.O. Box 603
Fort Erie, Ontario
L2A 5X3

HARLEQUIN
American Romance®

RELIVE THE MEMORIES....

From New York's immigrant experience to San Francisco's Great Quake of '06. From the western front of World War I to the Roaring Twenties. From the indomitable spirit of the thirties to the home front of the Fabulous Forties to the baby-boom fifties... A CENTURY OF AMERICAN ROMANCE takes you on a nostalgic journey.

From the turn of the century to the dawn of the year 2000, you'll revel in the romance of a time gone by and sneak a peek at romance in an exciting future.

Watch for all the CENTURY OF AMERICAN ROMANCE titles coming to you one per month over the next four months in Harlequin American Romance.

Don't miss a day of A CENTURY OF AMERICAN ROMANCE.

A CENTURY OF
AMERICAN ROMANCE
1960s

The women... the men... the passions... the memories...

REBECCA YORK

Labeled a "true master of intrigue" by *Rave Reviews*, best-selling author Rebecca York makes her Harlequin Intrigue debut with an exciting suspenseful new series.

It looks like a charming old building near the renovated Baltimore waterfront, but inside 43 Light Street lurks danger . . . and romance.

Let Rebecca York introduce you to:

> *Abby Franklin*—a psychologist who risks everything to save a tough adventurer determined to find the truth about his sister's death. . . .
>
> *Jo O'Malley*—a private detective who finds herself matching wits with a serial killer who makes her his next target. . . .
>
> *Laura Roswell*—a lawyer whose inherited share in a development deal lands her in the middle of a murder. And she's the chief suspect. . . .

These are just a few of the occupants of 43 Light Street you'll meet in Harlequin Intrigue's new ongoing series. Don't miss any of the 43 LIGHT STREET books, beginning with #143 LIFE LINE.

And watch for future LIGHT STREET titles, including #155 SHATTERED VOWS (February 1991) and #167 WHISPERS IN THE NIGHT (August 1991).

HI-143-1

HARLEQUIN *Temptation*

Give in to Temptation! Harlequin Temptation

The story of a woman who knows her own mind, her own heart . . . and of the man who touches her, body and soul.

Intimate, sexy stories of today's woman—her troubles, her triumphs, her tears, her laughter.

And her ultimate commitment to love.

Four new titles each month—get 'em while they're hot. Available wherever paperbacks are sold.

Temp-1